Book of the Film

This edition published by Parragon Books Ltd in 2016

Parragon Books Ltd
Chartist House
15–17 Trim Street
Bath BA1 1HA, UK
www.parragon.com

ISBN 978-1-4748-3639-5

Printed in UK

Book of the Film

Bath · New York · Cologne · Melbourne · Delhi
Hong Kong · Shenzhen · Singapore

"Hi, I'm Dory," the five-year-old blue tang fish said brightly. "I suffer from short-term memory loss."

Dory's giant eyes slowly blinked as she floated, waiting for a response. Her parents, Jenny and Charlie, clapped their fins with delight.

"Yes!" Jenny cheered.

"That's exactly what you say," said Charlie proudly.

Dory let out a happy sigh. Remembering things was very hard for the energetic little fish, so her parents often asked her to practise introducing herself.

The family lived in a charming coral home nestled safely behind a tall patch of sea grass. As the water's current moved, the sea grass waved gracefully.

"Okay, we'll pretend to be the other kids now," said Jenny. She and Charlie each took a deep breath as they attempted to get into character. "Hi, Dory," her mum said in a small voice.

"Ahoy there!" said Charlie in his best five-year-old voice. The sound of her parents pretending to be little fish made Dory giggle.

"Do you want to play hide-and-seek?" asked Charlie.

"Okay!" said Dory, tickled.

"We'll hide and you count and come find us," said Charlie.

"I'm hiding!" Jenny sang out from behind the sea grass.

Charlie turned to face his daughter. "Now count to ten," he said.

Dory placed her fins over her eyes and began to count while her father swam away. "One, two, three, um ... four ... um...." But that was as far as she got. Dory uncovered her eyes and looked around. She blinked and looked down, then rubbed her fins over the soft sand. She had already forgotten about the game.

"I like sand. Sand is squishy," she said, completely distracted by the sand.

Just then, Dory heard the sounds of children giggling in the distance. She peeked through the tall grass and saw a large school of young blue tangs playing together, swirling around like a ribbon and having a great time. Dory swam towards them. She wanted to play, too! But her parents quickly came out of their hiding places and stopped her before she could join in.

"Okay!" said Charlie. "Hide-and-seek might be a little advanced for right now."

Dory drew in a quick breath. "Mummy, can I go play with them?" she asked.

"Another time, honey," said Jenny gently. "Not until you're ready."

Dory saw her parents exchange a strained look that made her feel terrible. She never meant to disappoint them ... but it just kept happening.

"Did I forget again?" she asked sheepishly.

"No biggie, Kelpcake," said Charlie, trying to lighten the mood by calling Dory one of her many nicknames.

"Oh, sweetie, it's okay. Don't worry about it," said Jenny.

"What if I forget you?" asked Dory fearfully. Then she gasped. "Would you ever forget me?"

"Oh, Kelpcake, no," said Charlie.

"We will never forget you, Dory," added Jenny. "And we know you'll never forget us."

Dory smiled up at her parents as they both hugged her tightly.

A short time later, little Dory swam through the big, blue open water ... alone. She called out, searching for someone who might be able to help her.

"Hello...? Hello?"

"Did you hear that?" a fish asked her husband.

"Hellooooo!" young Dory's voice rang out again.

The wife followed the sound of Dory's voice. "Oh! There – right there!" She pointed her fin at the shape of a tiny fish in the distance. "I see a fish!"

"Well, it's the ocean," said her husband, Stan. "There are fish everywhere."

"Why do I swim with you?" the wife asked, exasperated. "HELLO?" she called again.

"Hello?" said Dory, pursuing the voices.

When they finally found each other, the couple was shocked to see a little fish swimming all by herself.

"Oh my goodness," said the wife. "It's a child!"

Dory was thrilled to see them. "Hi! I'm Dory! Can you please help me?" she asked.

"Well, hello, Dory," the wife answered. "Are you lost?"

"Where are your parents?" Stan asked.

"Um, I can't remember," said Dory.

"Okay," said Stan. "Well, we'll look around. Are any of these fish your parents?"

Dory slowly turned around, looking at the surrounding fish. She turned back to the couple and blinked. "Hi. I'm Dory. Can you please help me?"

The couple exchanged a look. "Dear, you told us that already," said the wife.

"I did?" asked Dory. "I'm sorry. I suffer from short-term memory loss."

"Oh, how awful," said the wife. She pulled her husband aside and asked him what he thought they should do. But when she turned back, Dory was gone! The couple swam around calling her name, trying to find her, but she had vanished.

Dory had already swum on and forgotten about the couple she had just met.

Alone and scared, Dory continued to search the strange waters. As the sun went down, the water became darker and scarier. Dory's eyes welled up with tears as she settled down under a rocky overhang. She softly sang, *"Just keep swimming.... Just keep swimming ... "* until she drifted off to sleep.

Years went by and Dory continued to ask for help from anyone who would listen. Most of the fish she ran into were sympathetic. They'd say things like "Really sorry we can't help you," or "Hope you find what you're looking for," or "Good luck." But how could anyone help her when she couldn't remember where she had come from? Or what she had lost in the first place? Dory searched and searched, but she'd completely forgotten everything. "I was looking for something," she said to one friendly fish. "I ... I just can't remember what." Dory patted her fins to her temples, hoping it would jog a memory into place. But nothing seemed to help.

Then one day, a boat streaked past overhead. The noisy engine caused other fish to scramble, but Dory stayed still, curiously watching as the boat went by. Suddenly, she heard a muffled, panicked voice in the distance and slowly swam towards it.

"A white boat!" the voice cried. "They took my son! My son! My son! Help me! Please!"

Out of nowhere, an upset clownfish appeared.

"Look out!" Dory screamed and then she smacked into him. He bounced off her and landed hard on the ocean floor.

"Sorry!" said Dory, concerned. "I didn't see you!"

The clownfish groaned as Dory inspected him.

"Are you okay?" Dory asked.

"He's gone!" the clownfish cried. He quickly introduced himself as Marlin. He continued to dash back and forth, worried out of his mind about his son.

Dory tried to comfort him again and again, but it didn't seem to help.

"No, no – they took him away. I have to find the boat!" Marlin said, swimming off.

"A boat? Hey, I've seen a boat!" said Dory.

"You have?" Marlin stopped and swam back to Dory.

"Uh-huh. This way. It went this way! Follow me!" Dory sped off and Marlin followed.

"Thank you! Thank you so much!" said Marlin, and they swam away together.

3

Dory and Marlin went on an incredible journey across the ocean to find Marlin's son, Nemo. A year passed, and after their grand adventure, Dory decided to stay with Marlin and Nemo – and join the community of the beautiful Great Barrier Reef. Dory had a cosy coral cave where she slept each night, and Marlin and Nemo lived in a comfy anemone only a few strokes away. Dory was able to remember more when they were together – in fact, everything seemed better now that they had each other. She, Marlin and Nemo were very close and they always tried to keep each other happy and safe.

One night, Dory swam out of her cave. Through the gentle swaying fronds of the sea anemone she could see Marlin and Nemo sleeping.

"Hey, Marlin," she whispered. She swam towards them and accidentally hit the anemone. It jolted her with an shock! "Ow-ow-ow-ow!" she cried.

Marlin awoke groggily and gently pushed her back into her cave. "Oh, Dory, it's not time to get up yet. You have to go back to bed."

"And remember, the anemone stings," Nemo said, still half asleep.

"Oh, right. Yeah. Sorry. Back to bed, back to bed," Dory said, settling back down. But she quickly headed out again, hitting the anemone's stinging cells again. "Ow!"

Now Marlin jumped up. "Go back to bed – that's it. Very simple. Bed. Back to it," he said curtly, pointing a fin towards her home.

"Ah. Um ... hmm. Got it," said Dory, once again swimming back to her cave. But then she turned around. "Hey, Marlin –"

"And we're up," said Marlin, realizing that he wouldn't be able to get back to sleep. "That's it. Ready to start the day."

Dory, Marlin and Nemo followed the winding path that led to Nemo's school. As they often did, they reminisced about their great adventure across the ocean to find Nemo.

"Okay," said Marlin. "So, there we were, stuck inside a whale, hanging from his tongue –"

"And we were looking for something," said Dory.

"Nemo," said Marlin.

"Hmm. Found him!" said Dory, smiling happily. "I remember it like it was yesterday. Although I don't really remember yesterday all that well," she admitted.

"That must have been the scariest part of the whole trip. Right, Dad?" Nemo asked.

"No, the scariest part of the whole trip was the four sharks."

Nemo looked at his father. "Wait, I thought there were *three* sharks."

"No," said Marlin. "No, there were definitely four."

"But last time you told it, there were three."

"Son, which one of us travelled across the entire ocean?"

"Nemo did," Dory said quickly. "Obviously, we had to cross the ocean to find him, so, you know ... he went first."

Marlin stared at Dory, realizing she was right. Nemo grinned proudly at his father. "I guess that's true, isn't it?" said Marlin, smiling.

When they got to Sandy Patch School, the teacher, Mr Ray, was pacing nervously. As Marlin, Dory and Nemo rounded the corner, Mr Ray swam towards them. "Weeeeell, you made it! You almost missed the field trip," the stingray said.

"A field trip? Ooh, I love field trips. Where are we going?" Dory asked excitedly.

Mr Ray gave Marlin a look. "I thought you told her," he whispered to Marlin.

"I did tell her," said Marlin. Then he turned to Dory. It was clear that he was going to have to explain the situation again.

"Uh, Dory ..." he said, trying to get her attention. Dory listened with a smile on her face. "Mr Ray has too many fish to keep an eye on today." Mr Ray swam off towards the class as Marlin continued. "So it would be best if – today – you weren't, exactly...." Marlin's voice trailed off as he tried to work out how to say what he needed to say without hurting Dory's feelings. Then he finished, "... with the class."

"Oh. Why not?" asked Dory.

"Well ... you know how you have problems

remembering things sometimes?" Marlin asked.

"That's the one thing I can remember, yes," Dory said with a chuckle.

"Okay, and sometimes – and it's not your fault – but it can cause you to wander," said Marlin.

"Mmm-hmm."

"So he doesn't have enough help. To keep an eye on ... on ... on those who are not –"

"Sure."

" – part of the group."

"Okay."

"He's ... he's a teacher, not a scout!" Marlin said, laughing nervously.

"Poor guy. You know, he is so overworked," said Dory.

Marlin wasn't sure that Dory was getting the full picture. "You understand?" Marlin asked.

"I totally understand now," she replied.

"Okay?"

"Um-hmm," said Dory.

"Good," Marlin said, satisfied.

"He wants me to be the teacher's assistant," Dory said proudly.

Marlin couldn't believe it! How could Dory get it so wrong? "Uh ... no, not exactly –"

"Well, I am so honoured. I have never been a teaching assistant before," said Dory happily.

Marlin sighed, giving up. "Mr Ray!" he called. "You've got help. Good luck!" Exasperated, Marlin swam back towards home.

"Ooohhkey-dokey," said Mr Ray.

Once the class settled, Mr Ray began his lesson. Dory tried to help in her own way ... by repeating everything he said.

"All right, kids!" said Mr Ray.

"All right, kids!" repeated Dory.

"Today's the day!" said Mr Ray.

"Today's the day!" repeated Dory.

"Our field trip to the stingray migration!"

"Stingray migration!"

"Now, does anyone know why we migrate?" asked Mr Ray.

No one responded. Mr Ray was met with blank stares and a deafening silence.

"Come on," said Dory, smacking her fins together. "You gotta know this stuff."

"Migration is about going back to ..." Mr Ray offered, trying to give the class a hint.

"Bed!" said Chickenfish.

"Yes!" said Dory.

"No," said Mr Ray.

"No!" echoed Dory.

"The sand!" answered Pearl, raising a fin.

"No," repeated Mr Ray. "Migration is about going home."

"Home," Dory repeated slowly. The word seemed to tug at something deep inside her.

"Which is where you're from," said Mr Ray.

"Where you're from ..." said Dory thoughtfully.

"Can someone tell me where they're from?" asked Mr Ray.

"I live by a giant rock!" yelled one student.

"My house is covered in algae!" yelled Chickenfish.

"Where'd you grow up, Dory?" asked a young crab.

"Me?" Dory asked, pointing her fin at her chest. "Um, I don't know ..." she said, her big eyes shifting downwards. The kids immediately quietened down; they were surprised by Dory's answer. "My family?" she continued. "Uh, where are they?" Dory turned and stared out at the open water, lost in thought. Something in that conversation had jogged her foggy memory. But she could never hold on to those thoughts for very long. When the water ceased to hold her attention, she turned to see Nemo's entire class staring at her.

"Can I help you?" she asked. They giggled. "I'm sorry." Dory was embarrassed. "Did I forget again? You see, I suffer from –"

The class chimed in together, "Short-term memory loss."

"What's it like having short-term memory loss?" asked Chickenfish.

"Good question," Dory answered. She thought for a moment, then tried to explain. "Well, like, for instance, if I'm thinking about ... say, kelp and then all of a sudden – what? And even though I just had the kelp in my head ... I ... see, I ... I don't even know what I said just now, to tell you the example. Let's just say it's kelp."

The class stared at Dory, bewildered, as she continued. She was forgetting right before their very eyes. "You say something about kelp and I'm like, what about kelp? But you're saying, 'You brought it up'. I'm like ... okay, that's gone now, too. I don't even know what we were just saying. See, that's my problem ... in a nutshell."

"Aw, that's so sad," said one young fish.

Dory smiled. "I try not to dwell on it," she said genuinely.

Mr Ray jumped in, eager to move on. "Okay, kids,

enough discussion. Climb aboard, explorers! I feel a migration song coming on!" He held a note as he sang, *"Ooooooooooohhhhhhhhhhhhhhhhhhh –"*

He continued to sing a migration song as he carried the class on his back. Dory sang along, swimming next to Mr Ray. When they reached the edge of the reef, the students jumped off and he reminded them to stay away from the edge.

The class settled down and waited expectantly.

"Now I need everyone to listen to me," started Mr Ray.

"All right, listen up!" said Dory, continuing to repeat Mr Ray's words.

"When the rays pass through here – what do we have to be careful of?" asked Mr Ray.

"Everybody has to be careful of what? Hmm?" echoed Dory.

"The undertow!" the students answered.

"That's right!" said Mr Ray.

"That's right, the under –" Dory said, stopping suddenly. "The undertow?" she said to herself. "I've heard that before."

Dory was so focused on the word that even as Mr Ray continued, his voice began to fade. Soon she didn't hear him at all.

"Mr Ray!" squealed Nemo, raising his fin. "So how do the stingrays all know where to go?" he asked.

"That's what instinct is, Nemo," answered Mr Ray. "Something deep inside you that feels so familiar that you have to listen to it – like a song you've always known." Mr Ray perked up and held a fin to his ear. "And I can hear mine now!"

In the distance, they heard the sound of many voices, singing as one. It was like a choir singing a beautiful song. As the stingrays swam closer, the choir became louder and louder. Everyone watched, amazed. The massive school of rays gracefully swam and sang in perfect harmony. It was an awesome sight!

The sea grass bent, pulled by the strength of the massive current created by the flapping of the rays' fins. But Dory just stared at the swaying grass. The way it moved reminded her of something. She slowly approached it, as if in a trance. Then, inside her mind, she heard a pair of faraway, frightened voices saying "Watch out, Kelpcake!" and "You have to stay away from the undertow!"

"The undertow," Dory said again, repeating that strangely familiar word. She drifted closer and closer to the rays and, all of a sudden, she was pulled into the undertow! She screamed as her body twirled and twisted – the whirling water was completely overtaking her!

"DORY!" shouted Nemo.

She continued to scream as she moved farther and farther away from Nemo and the rest of the class.

FLASH! Suddenly a lightning-fast clip of a memory played through her mind. She remembered being pulled away from her parents as they called her name. She heard their voices clearly shouting, again and again. Then everything went black.

4

"Dory? Dory!" Mr Ray said, peering over at her as she lay lifeless in the sand.

The kids gasped. "Is she dead?" asked Chickenfish, taking a closer look.

"No, she's not dead!" snapped Mr Ray. A few kids groaned, disappointed. "Give her some space, everybody."

Dory moved slightly and she started to murmur. Nemo leaned in, trying to decipher her words. It was difficult to understand what she was saying, but it sounded like 'Jewel of Morro Bay, California'.

Dory's eyes slowly fluttered open as Mr Ray, Nemo and the rest of the school class stared down at her.

"I remembered something," Dory gasped. In an instant, she was off the sea floor and frantically swimming in circles. "I remembered something! I actually remembered something! Something important!" She couldn't believe it. Dory had never experienced a memory before!

Later that day, when Marlin came to pick Dory and Nemo up from school, Dory was still confused and excited by her memory, even though she couldn't remember what it was. She scrunched up her face and batted her fins against her temples, trying as hard as she could to tap into it.

"Ugh ... I'm not sure anymore ... but I can still feel it. It's ... it's right there.... It's still in there...."

"All right," said Marlin, ready to head home. "Thank you, Mr Ray!"

Mr Ray and the class looked at each other, concerned, and watched as the three swam off.

With Marlin and Nemo following behind, Dory continued to strain, searching her mind for the hidden memory.

"Okay, c'mon. Try to remember better. Don't be

such a Dory, Dory!" she muttered, closing her eyes and pressing her fins against her temples. "Ahhh ... I don't remember.... It was something ... it was something about um, the um...."

"The Jewel of Morro Bay, California?" offered Nemo, repeating the phrase he thought he'd heard Dory say earlier.

Dory gasped and her eyes popped wide open as a flood of memories whipped through her mind. She heard young fish playing and laughing and saw her parents singing "Just keep swimming".

When she snapped back to the present moment, Dory raced ahead into the coral. "My family!" she said, thunderstruck. "My family! I REMEMBER MY FAMILY! They're out there somewhere! I have to find them! Guys, you gotta help me! Guys? Hello? Guys, where are you?"

"Dory!" shouted Marlin.

Dory was flustered. She anxiously looked around for Marlin and Nemo. "My parents! I remember them! My mum, my dad. I have a family!" said Dory excitedly. Then she gasped. "They don't know where I am. Let's go! We have to go!" Dory took off.

Marlin caught up to her and pulled her back.

"Dory, no! No! This is crazy! Where exactly are you trying to go?"

"To the – to the ... gem of the ... Baltic?"

"The Jewel of Morro Bay, California," said Nemo.

"Yes!" exclaimed Dory.

"No!" said Marlin. He continued to hold her back, preventing her from swimming away. "Dory, California's all the way across the ocean."

"Then we better get going! Come on!" she said, trying to break free from Marlin's grasp.

"How come every time we're on the edge of this reef, one of us is trying to leave? For once, can't we just enjoy the view?" Marlin asked, frustrated.

Dory finally wiggled free and she was upset. "How can you be talking about the view when I remembered my family?" She raced away again, but Marlin intercepted and slowly pushed her back to the safety of the reef.

"No, no! We've done our ocean travels. That part of our lives is over. The only reason you travel in the first place is so you don't have to travel ever again," said Marlin firmly.

Then he lost his grip on Dory and slipped, falling face-first into the sand. He coughed, spitting sand out of his mouth.

"Please," said Dory. "All I know is that I miss them. I really, really miss them. I didn't know what that felt like.... Do you know what that feels like?" She stared straight into Marlin's eyes.

Marlin sighed and looked over at Nemo. He remembered how much his heart ached when Nemo had got lost the year before. "Yes," he said softly. "I know what that feels like."

Dory looked out at the vast open water sadly and Marlin's heart broke for his dear friend. He wouldn't wish that feeling on anyone.

"I don't want to forget this," said Dory. "Somewhere – out there – is my family. Please, Marlin. I can't find them on my own. I'll forget. Please help me find my family."

"Yeah, Dad," said Nemo. "You can get us all the way across the ocean, right?"

"No," Marlin said, and their faces fell. "But I know a guy."

5

"**W**oo-hoo!" shouted Crush, Marlin's sea turtle friend. He wore a huge smile as he cruised through the choppy water carrying Dory, Marlin and Nemo on his shell. "Righteous! Righteous chop! Righteous chop!" he yelled, laughing. A crew of little sea turtles swam expertly along with them.

Marlin clung to the front of Crush's shell. "Totally sick! Totally siiiiiick!" he said.

Crush turned to Marlin and smiled. "I know. Isn't it great?"

"No!" said Marlin, his face turning green. "I'm gonna be totally sick."

"It's the California current, dude. Got some gnarly chop! SURF'S UP, DUDE!" yelled Crush.

Marlin screamed as Crush quickly rose and fell, riding each ripple of the choppy water. Marlin then made a horrible gagging noise as he hung on to the turtle's shell for dear life.

"Hey, dude, if you're gonna hurl, just do me a solid: head to the back of the shell, lean out and go for distance!" said Crush.

One of the small turtles, Squirt, said, "We call that feeding the fishes!"

"Correctomundo, slightly older Squirt!" said Crush happily.

At the back of the shell, Dory was telling some of the younger turtles her story. "Now we're looking for my parents at the, um, the ... Brooch of the Atlantic? Or the – no, no – The Bauble of the ..."

"The Jewel of Morro Bay, California!" said Nemo proudly, reminding her.

"Exactly!" said Dory.

"But how are you going to find your parents?" asked one of the young turtles.

"Do you remember what they look like?" asked little Squirt.

"I'm a bit new to the memory thing, so I can't say for sure, but something tells me they were mostly blue with a little bit of yellow," Dory answered.

"That sounds right," said Nemo, smiling.

"Also, I'm pretty sure they're going to be looking for me, because they said they'd never forget me," said Dory.

The turtles rode the waves as the current helped to carry them across the ocean.

"Morro Bay, California's coming up, dudes!" shouted Crush.

"WOO-HOO! LET'S FIND MY FAMILY!" Dory cried excitedly.

"Go! Go! Go!" shouted Crush.

"Just go, Dad!" yelled Nemo.

"Don't push me, Nemo –" Marlin screamed as he fell off Crush's shell.

Dory and Nemo eagerly jumped off, cheering and laughing as Marlin groaned, feeling extremely sick. They tumbled out of the current and watched as the turtles continued on, swimming into the distance.

"So long, Dory-dude! Hope you find your parents!" shouted Squirt.

"And good luck feedin' the fishes!" said Crush as he sped away.

Marlin slowly picked up his head. "Too late," he moaned. "Already fed."

The three floated for a moment as they looked

around at their surroundings. It was oddly still and quiet. An enormous sunken container ship seemed to rise eerily from the sand, like a ruined city. Its containers, pieces of junk and rubbish were scattered around the ocean floor, covered with years of coral and algae growth.

"This feels familiar," Dory said. Then she raced off, calling out for her parents: "Mum! Dad!"

"Dory, Dory, Dory. Wait!" said Marlin, chasing after her. But she continued to shout. "Dory!" Marlin said again, firmly. "Stop yelling for a second. Do you really think your parents are just going to be floating around here, waiting for you?"

"Well, only one way to find out," she said, then shouted, "Mum! Dad!" at the top of her lungs, searching.

"Yell louder, Dory!" said Nemo.

"MUM!" shouted Dory, even louder. "DAD!"

Various pieces of rubbish littered around the ship rustled and came to life as a chorus of whispers demanded quiet. "Shhh!"

"What was that?" asked Nemo, looking around fearfully.

It was a community of hermit crabs! But just as the friends caught a tiny glimpse of the crabs, the crabs disappeared, hiding beneath the rusty cans, warped pipes and plastic cups on their backs. Dory's mind raced as she experienced a strange feeling.

"Wait, I've heard that before," she said. "I remember somebody saying, 'Shhh'."

"Yes, well done," said Marlin sarcastically. "That was me, one minute ago, telling you to be quiet –"

"SHHHHHH!" the hermit crabs whispered forcefully, popping up long enough to urgently shush them again.

FLASH! Another memory rushed through Dory's mind!

She could see herself as a young fish, swimming by the sunken container ship. The very same hermit crabs shushed her! She asked the hermit crabs for help. "Have you seen my Mummy and Daddy? Their names are Jenny and Charlie."

"SHHHHH!" the hermit crabs said.

The memory left as quickly as it had zipped into her mind: Dory was back in the present moment. "Jenny and Charlie," she said to herself.

"What?" asked Marlin.

Dory's eyes widened with excitement. "THOSE ARE THEIR NAMES! MY PARENTS ARE JENNY AND CHARLIE!" Dory cheered. She darted ahead, swimming deeper into the containers, calling for her parents as loudly as she could. "JENNY? CHARLIE? JENNY? CHARLIE?"

"Dory, *wait!*" said Marlin, chasing after her. "Again with the frantic yelling. Can we just take a moment and come up with a plan?"

The hermit crabs jumped out of hiding and shushed them again as they swam past, but Dory continued to call her parents' names.

"Are you crazy?" asked one of the crabs.

"Sorry," said Marlin. "She's a little excited."

Marlin and Nemo caught up with Dory, who was still screaming as loudly as she could.

"Dory, stop yelling for a second!" said Marlin. "It's not a good idea to come into a new neighborhood and call this much attention to yourself. These crabs are locals and I get the feeling they're shushing us for a reason –"

Grrrrrr! A loud roar sounded from the shipping container and all the crabs dropped down, disappearing once again beneath their cans, pipes and cups.

"Aaaand there's our reason," said Marlin.

"Mummy?" asked Dory, turning towards the container.

An enormous eye popped open and stared at them through a porthole window in the container. The deafening roar sounded again and a giant squid rose out of hiding! Dory, Marlin and Nemo screamed and swam away as fast as they could.

"That is *definitely* not Mummy!" shouted Dory.

They turned abruptly, swimming as fast as they could to escape the giant squid. They ducked into a different container, dipping and dodging various obstacles. There was rubbish everywhere, including a six-pack ring that entangled the three of them. While they tried to escape, the ring hugged their bodies, making it difficult to swim. Marlin and Nemo managed to escape the plastic, but the ring was still wrapped around Dory as the squid chased them through another towering stack of containers.

"Swim for your life!" screamed Marlin.

They slipped through a crack in one of the containers, but the squid squeezed through, right behind them. The friends squashed themselves through a hole that was too big for the squid, thankfully. The squid wrestled with the containers, causing a pile of them to start crumbling. One by one, the containers came crashing down. But in the scuffle, the squid reached out a giant tentacle and grabbed Nemo!

"Nemo!" Marlin and Dory screamed, clutching him tightly.

"Dad!" Nemo shouted. The squid was bringing him towards its mouth!

"Nemo, hold on to me!" Marlin urged. "And don't let go!"

Finally, the squid lost its grip. At the same time, the container hit the ground. The impact propelled Dory, Marlin and Nemo into the safety of a kelp forest.

Marlin rushed to Nemo. "Are you all right?"

Nemo was crying and trembling with fear.

"Oh my goodness, Nemo!" said Dory, concerned. "Are you okay? What happened?"

Marlin held up his fin and stayed focused on Nemo. "Not now, Dory. Please."

Dory paced, swimming around in a big circle. When she came back and saw Nemo, she was concerned all over again. "Oh my goodness, Nemo! Are you okay?"

"I said not now," Marlin uttered, his jaw clenched. "You've done enough."

"But I can fix it. I'll go get help –" said Dory.

"You know what you can do, Dory?" said Marlin, frustrated. "You can wait over there. Go wait over there and forget." Then he muttered under his breath, "It's what you do best."

Hurt, Dory backed away. "I'm so sorry," she said quietly.

"No, Dad," said Nemo. "I'm okay."

"I'm gonna get help, okay? I can do that." Dory swam off and called back to them, "It'll be all right, Nemo!"

As Marlin and Nemo continued to recover from the scary encounter with the squid, they didn't see Dory swim away. She swam around, searching. "Hello? Someone? Hello?"

Swimming upwards, she heard a voice echoing from above. "Hello," said the voice.

"Hello?" Dory carried on towards it.

The voice continued to speak.

"Oh! I need your help," said Dory, swimming even closer.

"Won't you please join us," said the voice.

"Oh! Great!" said Dory, swimming up to the surface, searching for the voice.

"... as we explore the wonders of the Pacific Ocean and the amazing life it holds within. Witness the majesty of the beluga whale," the voice continued.

"Where are you?" asked Dory, frantically looking around for whoever was speaking.

When Marlin and Nemo realized that Dory had left them, they raced off to find her.

"There you are!" shouted Marlin when he saw her.

"Guys! I found help!" cried Dory.

"Look out!" shouted Marlin, as Dory was suddenly lifted out of the water by a pair of human hands.

The humans gently brought Dory into their boat. "Oh, look at this!" said one of them, eyeing the six-pack ring, which was still strung around her.

"No respect for ocean life," said the other, disgusted.

Nemo and Marlin watched in horror as the humans inspected Dory and removed the plastic.

"Marlin! Nemo!" Dory shouted.

"No, no, no! Not again!" said Marlin.

The humans put Dory in a cooler and shut the lid.

"Let's take her inside and see how she does," said one of the humans. Then the boat took off and headed towards the shore.

"Don't worry, Dory!" yelled Marlin. "Stay calm! We'll come find you!"

As Marlin and Nemo called after the boat, the voice that Dory had been following echoed in the distance: "Welcome to the Marine Life Institute, where we believe in rescue, rehabilitation and release."

And just like that ... Dory was gone.

6

"**M**arlin will come find me. Marlin will come find me," Dory chanted in the dark. Suddenly, the light streamed in as the lid of the cooler was opened and she was dropped into a small tank. Dory paced as she looked around. She noticed the room was full of tanks.

Two marine centre workers approached and one plunged a net into Dory's tank. "I'm glad we found this one." The other reached his hand in and clipped an orange tag to Dory's fin.

"Huh? What's happening? Help!" groaned Dory, as the two workers left the room.

Dory didn't notice that behind her, an inspirational poster on the wall had come to life! A large orange, seven-legged octopus emerged from the picture. He had camouflaged himself to look like a kitten holding on to a rope.

Dory continued to pace nervously as the octopus slinked over to her tank. He watched her spin a few times before reaching in and suctioning himself to her tag.

"Hey, you. Spinner!" he said.

"Oh, thank goodness!" said Dory. "Hi, I'm Dory."

"Name's Hank," he said. Then he looked at her. "How sick are you?"

"Sick?" Dory asked, alarmed. "I'm sick?"

"Why else would you be in Quarantine?"

"Oh, no. How long do I have? I have to find my family!" said Dory.

"All right, now – don't get hysterical," he said gruffly. Then he spotted her tag. "Uh-oh. Not good."

"What is it? What happened?" Dory asked anxiously.

Hank pointed to her tag and Dory turned to see it. She gasped. "What's that?"

"That there is bad news," said Hank. "It's a transport tag – for fish who can't cut it inside the Institute. They get transferred to permanent digs. An aquarium." Then Hank leaned in and whispered gravely, "In Cleveland."

"Cleveland?" Dory said, gasping. "No, I can't go to the Cleveland! I have to get to the Jewel of Morro Bay, California and find my family –"

"That's this place," said Hank, interrupting her. "The Marine Life Institute. The Jewel of Morro Bay, California. You're here."

Dory couldn't believe it! "You mean I'm from here?" Then it dawned on her. "I'm from here!" she repeated.

Hank tapped on the glass of her tank. "So, what exhibit are you from?"

"Wait, I'm from an exhibit? Which one? I have to get there."

Hank sighed. "That's a hard one, kid. Unless...." His voice trailed off. Then he said, "Nah, it'd never work. It's too crazy."

"What do you mean? Just tell me! I'm okay with crazy," said Dory.

"You know, I could see that," Hank agreed. "Well, there's one thing I can think of to help you get to your family." He started moving one of his tentacles towards the tag on her fin. "If I just take –"

Dory suddenly moved out of reach. "Yes! Great idea! You take me to find them! Why didn't I think of that?"

"Uh – no. If I just take your tag, I can take your place on the transport truck. Then you can go back inside and find your family. All you have to do is give me the tag."

"What tag?" Then Dory gasped. "There's a tag on my fin!"

Hank squinted, trying to figure her out. "How could you forget you have a tag on your fin?" he asked, confused.

"Oh, no. I'm sorry. I suffer from short-term memory loss," Dory explained.

"You don't remember what we were talking about?" asked Hank.

"Not a clue. What were we talking about?" asked Dory.

Hank thought for a moment and saw an opportunity to get what he wanted. "You were about to give me your tag," he said.

"Well, I kinda like my tag. Why do you want it?"

"So I CAN GO TO –" Hank paused, wrapping his tentacles around the tank to pull it closer. Then he whispered, "So I can go to Cleveland." He was getting frustrated.

"Cleveland? Hmm. I hear good things about Cleveland. Why do you want to go?" asked Dory.

"Because if I stay here, I'm gonna get released back to the ocean! And I have extremely unpleasant memories of that place! I just want to live in a glass box, alone. It's all I want!" Hank said, reaching for her tag. "So give me your tag!"

Dory flicked him away. "Hey, man, don't touch my tag."

Hank sighed. He slumped into the sink, looked around and spotted a coffeepot. He grabbed it and guzzled down the little bit of coffee that was left inside.

"Look. I don't work here. It's not like I have a map of this place," he said.

"A map," said Dory. "Great! You can take me to a map and I can figure out where my parents are. Oh, boy."

"All right. If I get you to your family, will you give me —"

"I don't have much.... Um ... how about if I give you this tag?" she offered.

Hank stuck the empty coffeepot into Dory's tank and scooped her up along with some water. "Great idea," he said sarcastically. Then he carried the coffeepot towards the door, with Dory swishing inside.

7

Outside the Institute, Marlin was freaking out.

"Are you absolutely sure that's what I said? 'Go wait over there and forget. It's what you do best'?"

"Yeah, Dad," said Nemo.

"I said that?" he asked again.

"You said that, Dory swam to the surface and then she got taken –"

"All right, I don't need the whole story again, I was asking about one part." Marlin was pacing back and forth as he talked. "Because look, if I said that – I'm not positive I did – but it's actually a compliment. Because I asked her to wait. I didn't say leave. And I said it's what you do *best*."

42

Nemo looked at his Dad incredulously.

"It's my fault!" Marlin threw his fins in the air. "It's all my fault Dory got kidnapped and taken into – whatever this place is! What if it's a restaurant?" he worried.

Marlin yelled so loud that a couple of plump sea lions, Fluke and Rudder, woke up with a snort. They'd been sleeping on a nearby rock and were not happy to be disturbed.

"Oi! You two! Shut it!" Fluke shouted.

"Yeah, we're trying to sleep," Rudder said. "And you interrupted my favourite dream!"

"The one about you layin' on this rock?" asked Fluke.

"Yeah."

"Oh, that's a good one."

"Uh, excuse us?" said Nemo. "Hello. We're trying –"

Marlin cut him off. "Son, son, son ..." he whispered, trying to scoot Nemo away. "These are sea lions. They are natural predators. They could pounce at any moment!" One of the sea lions stretched open his mouth and let out a big, lazy yawn.

"They don't look very pouncy," said Nemo.

"That's what they want you to think. Just get behind me and let me do the talking," Marlin said.

He cleared his throat and approached the sea lions. "Excuse me. We're worried about our friend. Is that a restaurant?" Marlin pointed to the large building behind the rock.

"Nah, mate, it's not a restaurant," said Fluke, chuckling. "Your friend is okay."

"She is?" asked Marlin.

"It's a fish hospital. She'll be rescued, rehabilitated and released," said Fluke.

"Yeah, she'll be in and out in a jiff," said Rudder. "We should know."

They lifted their tails to show tags that had been clipped on.

"Nasal parasite," said Fluke, explaining.

"Anemia," said Rudder.

"All fixed up and sent on our way," said Fluke.

Marlin was relieved. "Oh, thank goodness."

"Sure, that's right, don't you worry about –"

Suddenly, a skinny sea lion carrying a green pail in his mouth appeared behind them, giggling and creeping up the rock.

"Gerald! Get off the rock! Off! Off! Off! Off!" Fluke barked.

"Oy!" yelled Rudder. "Shove off, Gerald!"

Rudder and Fluke continued to yell, scaring Gerald

away from the rock and causing him to jump back into the ocean.

Once he was gone, Fluke and Rudder turned back to Marlin.

"Don't you worry," Fluke continued. "That place is the Marine Life Institute: the Jewel of Morro Bay, California," he said.

"She was right!" said Nemo. "Well, Dad, looks like Dory can do something besides forget."

"Thank you, Nemo," said Marlin sarcastically. "Thank you for that."

"So how are we gonna get inside?" asked Nemo.

"Oh, wait. You want to get inside the MLI?" asked Rudder.

"Desperately! Our friend is in there, lost, alone. She's scared. She'll have no idea what to do," said Marlin.

"Oh," said Fluke with a smirk. "We know a way."

"You do?" asked Marlin.

All of a sudden, Fluke and Rudder began cooing. *"Oo-roo. Ooo-roo-rooo!"*

"What are they doing?" asked Nemo.

"I don't know," said Marlin. "It sounds bad."

8

Inside the Institute, Hank carried Dory in the coffeepot down an empty hallway.

"Hank, I am so glad I found you," Dory whispered. "It feels like ... destiny!"

"Shhh," said Hank, annoyed. "For what must be the millionth time, it's not destiny."

"Have I said 'destiny' before?" asked Dory. "I'm sorry. I think I'm so nervous because I'm gonna meet my parents. I haven't seen them in ... I don't even know how long, because, well, you see, I suffer from –"

"Short-term memory loss!" said Hank, interrupting her. He was fed up of hearing Dory repeat herself.

"Look, no more talking, okay? I don't like talking. I don't like chatter and questions and" – Hank put on a pretend voice – "'How are you?' 'Oh, I'm fine. How are you?' 'Oh I'm fine, too.' News flash: NOBODY'S FINE!"

A phone rang in the distance. They heard a voice answer the call. "Oh, I'm fine. How are you?"

Hank grimaced. He'd heard it a million times and he didn't believe it. He peered around the corner and saw the member of staff on the phone at his desk.

Dory gazed out into the hallway. "Hank, look!" she said. A framed map of the Institute hung on the wall across from the worker's office. "There's a map!"

"Shhh. The plan is you're gonna read that and figure out where your parents live," said Hank. "Then I'm on the truck to Cleveland. You got it?"

"Got it," said Dory. "What was that first part again?"

"Just read the map," said Hank curtly. He quietly moved towards it and lifted Dory to give her a closer look.

"Look at all the exhibits," she said, impressed. "How can you do this park in one day? Seriously."

"Pick one," whispered Hank, furious.

While Dory scanned the map, the member of staff rolled his chair into the doorway of his office and sighed. He was still on the phone and obviously annoyed. "Really, Jerrie, I can't believe I actually convinced Mum to hire you. How hard is it to find an octopus?" he said into the receiver. As he leaned back in the chair, the worker looked directly at Hank and Dory! But Hank had instantly camouflaged himself, holding the coffeepot in such a way that it looked like Dory was part of the map's design. The worker had no idea that anything was out of place!

"Of course I haven't seen him," the worker continued. "If I was looking, I'd find him...." He then rolled his chair back towards his desk and out of view.

Hank let out a hefty sigh as he came out of his camouflage.

"Hank! There you are," said Dory.

"Hurry up!" Hank whispered.

Dory read the map. "Maybe they live in the Kid Zone! That's where I'd live."

"No, no kids!" Hank exclaimed. "Kids grab things and I'm not losing another tentacle for you!"

"You lost a tentacle?" Dory asked. "Well, then, you're not an octopus. You're a septopus. I may not remember, but I can count."

"Hurry up!" Hank said again. He was running out of patience.

Dory went back to reading the map and stopped when she saw a picture of a purple shell. "Hey, look. Shells," Dory said.

Suddenly, another memory flashed in her mind!

Dory saw herself as a child, looking around in the sand with her parents.

"Hey, look. Shells!" said little Dory. "Daddy, here's a shell for you!"

"That's great, Dory!" said Charlie. "You found another one."

"I did?"

"Yes, you did," said Jenny. "You're getting good at this."

Little Dory watched her father place the shells in a line. The shells led to the door of their coral home.

"Hey, look. Shells," Dory said again.

Jenny chuckled as little Dory followed the shell path towards her door. "Hey, I live here," she said.

"Yes — yes indeed," said Charlie.

"I like shells," said Dory.

"That's right, dear," said Jenny with a giggle. "Do you think you could find me another shell? Purple ones are my favourite."

Little Dory looked around the yard and noticed a purple shell just beyond the grass fence. "Mummy, look! Purple shells!" she said, heading towards the fence.

Then everything in the memory seemed to shake and quiver. And just like that, Dory was back in the present moment.

"Purple shells! Purple sh –" Dory paused, trying to catch her breath. "Hank, my home had a purple shell!" she said excitedly.

"So what? Half the exhibits here have purple shells in them."

"No, no – you don't understand! I remember her now! Purple shells were her favourite! And she had this adorable giggle. And my dad was really friendly," Dory said.

Suddenly, they heard footsteps clicking along the hallway. Someone was coming!

"And now your wacky memory's gonna get us caught," said Hank.

Hank quickly rushed down the hall, using all seven tentacles to move rapidly across the floor. Thinking fast, he slinked behind a door to hide. Then the worker, who was carrying a bucket, appeared and walked straight towards them!

"Still think this is destiny?" Hank whispered.

Before Dory could answer, the worker came through the door! Screaming, Hank slithered out of the way. When the worker got to the bottom of the stairs, she spotted the slime trail. "Ugh," she groaned. "That octopus is out again? All right, where are you?" She put down her bucket and started looking around.

Hank camouflaged himself again, disappearing as he wound himself around the stairway railing. "See what you did?" he whispered harshly to Dory. "This could not be worse!"

The worker's bucket caught Dory's eye and she gasped as she read the word printed on it: DESTINY! While the worker continued to search for Hank, Dory was struck with an idea. "Hank! I got a feeling. I think we should get in the bucket."

"No, stop," whispered Hank nervously.

"Seriously. It says 'Destiny', and it is."

"No, no, no, no, no!" Hank protested.

"We've gotta get in that bucket," Dory said defiantly. Hank refused, but Dory insisted.

"Don't you jump in that bucket!" Hank warned.

Dory geared up to jump. Hank tried to stop her, but she ignored him and tipped the coffeepot over, slipping and landing safely inside her destination – the Destiny bucket.

Dory swam among dozens of floating silver fish. "Hey, guys?" Dory said. "I'm looking for my family." The fish turned their bellies up, lifeless. "Oh, good idea," said Dory. "Play dead."

The worker, unable to find Hank, finally gave up. She sighed, picked up her bucket and started off.

Dory swayed from side to side, moving with the water as the worker carried her along. "Oh, you guys are good. I gotta blink," Dory said to the silver fish. "How do you hold your eyes open that long?"

Hank panicked, watching the worker walk away and immediately took off after them. But the worker walked so fast that he couldn't keep up. He quickly scanned the room to survey his options. He curled his tentacles around one of the ceiling pipes and thrust himself through the air – swinging from pipe to pipe – and made up for lost time. When the worker reached the door, Hank tried to jump into the bucket. But his timing was off! He missed the bucket and smacked into the door, which the worker had closed behind her.

Inside the bucket, Dory was still whispering to the fish floating around her. "Hey, guys?"

But the fish just bobbed up and down lifelessly. She poked one of them, then realized something was very wrong. "Wait a second –" But before she could finish her thought, the worker's hand dipped into the bucket and grabbed Dory, along with a handful of the floating fish – and tossed them into the air! Dory screamed as she plunged into a giant pool.

9

Dory tumbled through the water and bumped into the glass enclosing an undersea exhibit. She blinked her big eyes and saw a group of children on the other side. They stared at her as their tour continued.

"Our next guest has been here a very long time. She's a whale shark," said the tour guide. "Her name is Destiny."

"Destiny?" said Dory with surprise. "Really?"

"You'll notice she's extremely nearsighted and has trouble navigating her environment – oh! Here she comes now!" said the guide, turning towards the glass.

A giant whale shark entered from the other side of the pool. She weaved uneasily, this way and that, as she swam towards Dory with squinted eyes. "Destiny!" said Dory. "You're a fish?"

"Wait … what?" Destiny said and swam haphazardly through the tank as she strained even harder in an effort to see. She swerved at the last minute to avoid hitting Dory and the glass.

"Can you help me?" Dory asked. "Whoa," she said when Destiny nearly crashed into her. "All right, I'll go with you." She followed Destiny and tried to get her attention while Destiny zigzagged around the tank. "Excuse me? Hi. Can I just speak to you for a sec?"

Unfortunately, Destiny was distracted. She continued to twist and contort her face, trying to see clearly enough to avoid the walls. She was always crashing into them. "I got it … I got it … I got this … I…." Destiny said. But she quickly lost confidence and began to panic. "Where's the wall? Where's the wall?" Destiny asked frantically. She was heading straight towards the viewing glass! The tourists on the other side began to panic, too!

At the last moment, Dory took Destiny's fin and righted her. Dory smiled and waved as Destiny opened her eyes, sighing with relief. With Dory's help, she'd avoided the crash.

"Excuse me –" said Dory.

"Who is that?" asked Destiny, squinting. "Is that blue blob talking?"

"Can you help me? I lost my family and –"

"You lost your family?" Destiny asked.

"Well, it's a long story and truth be told, I don't remember most of it," Dory admitted.

"Oh, that is so sad! You poor –" Destiny rammed into a wall. "Sorry. I'm not a great swimmer. Can't see very well."

"Oh, I think you swim beautifully," said Dory. "In fact, I've never seen a fish swim like that before."

"*ThAAnk yooOoou!*" she said, speaking in whale.

"*Yooooouuuuuuu're weeeeeeeelcoooooooome!*" Dory answered in whale.

"Wait. Say that again," said Destiny.

"You're welcome!" Dory repeated.

Destiny paused for a moment. "Dory?" she asked, her eyes growing wide. She recognized this fish! "You and I were friends!"

"You know me?" asked Dory. She swam close to one of Destiny's eyes so the whale shark could take a closer look.

"Aw, you're so pretty!" Destiny said. Then she lost her balance and sank towards the bottom of the pool. But Dory stayed with her. "Of course I know you!" Destiny continued. "We'd talk through the pipes when we were little. You from your exhibit, me from here. We were pipe pals!"

"We were?" asked Dory, confused.

"It was so much fun, because I'd tell you a story and then you'd completely forget about it. And then I'd get to tell it to you over and over again. Do you know what I'm talking about?"

"No. Well," Dory paused. "I don't remember."

Destiny reached the bottom of the pool upside down and stayed there, chatting with Dory. "Yes! See, that's what I'm talking about! Oh, it's so great to finally meet you!" said Destiny happily.

"So you know where I'm from?" Dory asked.

"Yeah," said Destiny. "The Open Ocean exhibit."

Dory was thrilled! "Can you take me there?" she quickly asked.

"Uh ... kinda tough for a whale to travel around here," said Destiny.

She started to look around and realized she was upside down. Dory offered Destiny her fin again and helped the big fish turn the right way up.

"So you're a whale?" asked Dory.

"Uh ... whale shark, to be exact. But let's be honest, who likes sharks?"

Suddenly, Bailey, a beluga whale, appeared at a gate that divided the two pools. "Can you please keep it down over there?" complained Bailey. "My head hurts."

Destiny sighed. "That's my neighbour, Bailey," she whispered. She explained that he had been brought to the Institute because of a head injury.

"I know you're talking about me, Destiny," snapped Bailey.

Bailey tried to move around to get a better view, but Destiny raised and lowered her fins, blocking him. "He thinks he can't use his echolocation, but I've overheard the doctors talking. There's not a thing wrong with him."

"I'm right here. I hear every word you're saying," said Bailey.

"What's echolocation?" asked Dory.

Destiny turned and faced Bailey. "Well, Bailey's head is supposed to put out a call and the echo helps him find objects that are far away. Oh, but apparently he's still 'healing'," Destiny said.

"Now I *know* you're talking about me," said Bailey.

"I really can't echolocate."

"Oh, I cannot have this conversation again. I just can't," said Destiny with a sigh.

"I hit my head very hard out there. See how swollen it is?" said Bailey, showing off his bulging head.

"Your head is *supposed* to be big! You're a *beluga*!" said Destiny.

"Echo-lo-cation," said Dory, puzzling over the word. "Oh! Like the world's most powerful pair of glasses?"

"What?" asked Destiny.

"What are glasses?" asked Bailey.

"It's sort of like you go '*OoooOOOoooOoooh*' and then you see things," Dory said, pretending to echolocate. She paused for a moment. "Why do I know that?" she asked herself.

"Oh, that's interesting," said Bailey stiffly. He whispered to Destiny, "Your friend is weird."

A pool toy splashed into the water, catching their attention. The toy unexpectedly transformed right before their eyes into ... Hank! He swam over to Dory. "There you are!" he shouted. "You and I are square," he said firmly.

"Hank –"

"I took you to the map –"

Dory excitedly told Hank that she'd found out where she was from.

"Open Ocean?" said Hank. "I know where that is. That's the exhibit located right next to" – he leaned in and whispered – "I don't care."

Destiny told Dory she could get to the Open Ocean exhibit through the pipes. "Take two lefts, swim straight and you'll hit it."

"Oooh, that's a lot of directions," said Dory nervously. "Did you get that, Hank? All that?"

But Hank wasn't interested. "I'm not going with you," he said. "I won't fit. You have to go by yourself."

Dory was afraid. She didn't trust herself to remember the right way to go. "I'm not so good with directions."

"Well, that's too bad," said Hank. "A deal's a deal. You want to get to your parents – that's how you get to 'em," he continued, sticking out a tentacle and pointing towards the pipes. "Now give me your tag!"

"But, Hank, I can't go into the pipes alone. I'll just forget where I'm going," Dory pleaded.

"Not my problem," said Hank. He jutted out another tentacle and yelled, "Tag!"

"But I can't get in that way!" yelled Dory.

"Well, I'm sorry, but there's no other way!"

"There's no other way," said Dory quietly.

FLASH! Another memory popped into her head.

She could see the grass entrance outside her childhood home as her younger self tried to pull up a shell that was buried deep in the sand.

"There's no other way," little Dory said, ready to give up.

"Don't panic," said Charlie, swimming over to her.

"It's okay," said Jenny. "Not everything in life is easy to do. Isn't that right, Charlie?"

"That's right. When something's too hard, Dory, you should just give up," said Charlie.

Jenny was startled. "Charlie! How can you – ?"

"A joke. I'm kidding! Just a joke…. Caution! Joker at work!" he said, chuckling.

"Oh, honey. Oh, a joke, I got it," said Jenny, relieved.

Charlie used his tail to wiggle the shell and pry it out of the sand. It popped right out and little Dory joyfully plopped inside. Charlie pushed Dory and the shell back towards their coral cave house, lining it up with a bunch of others.

"See, Kelpcake," said Charlie, smiling. "There's always another way."

Charlie hugged little Dory tightly as she giggled.

The memory vanished when Dory opened her eyes. She was hugging Hank's tentacle as Hank tried to sneak the tag off her fin!

"Nope," said Dory. "My father said, 'There's always another way.'" She quickly headed for the surface as Hank chased after her. Dory scanned the area and Destiny pointed out the Open Ocean building over the hill.

"Open Ocean. It's that building right there. The one that looks like Bailey's head."

Bailey surfaced. "Wait, what?"

Then Hank surfaced. "There is absolutely *no other* w –"

Dory pointed to a rack of baby pushchairs in the distance, across from Destiny's pool.

"There!" she shouted, interrupting Hank. "We're gonna use one of those and take it across the park to locomotion," said Dory.

"Open Ocean," said Bailey and Destiny together, correcting her.

"Exactly," said Dory.

10

Outside the Marine Life Institute, Marlin and Nemo were wondering how they were going to get inside. Fluke and Rudder were still *"Ooo-roo-ing,"* and things were looking hopeless.

"What are you doing?" Marlin asked. "What is that?"

"Calling her over, of course," said Fluke.

"Calling who?" asked Marlin.

Almost instantly, a flock of sea birds landed nearby. The birds parted to reveal a wacky-looking one.

"Lads, meet Becky," said Fluke.

Rudder spoke to her in her own language and she responded with a loud *SQUAWK*!

"Flying?" screamed Marlin. "No, no, no, no new information. Listen, tell her thank you. I mean, you guys have gone above and beyond, really. But is there a way to get in that involves water? Like swimming? Because that's really our strength."

"Look, your friend is going to be in Quarantine. That's where they take the sick fish," explained Fluke.

"And the one – and only one – way into that place ... is Becky!" said Rudder.

Becky squawked again, landing right behind Marlin and Nemo.

Marlin jumped, laughing nervously. "Hi, Becky."

Becky started to peck Marlin. "I think she likes you, Dad," said Nemo.

"Becky, love?" said Fluke. Becky stopped pecking and looked up at Rudder and Fluke, curiously cocking her head. "These two nice fish need to get into Quarantine," said Fluke.

"Are you free today, Rebecca darling?" asked Rudder.

Becky cooed as she looked at Marlin.

"Becky is, uh ... would that work with your schedule?" Marlin asked awkwardly. Becky began pecking at Marlin again.

"Ow!" Marlin screamed. "She doesn't understand what I'm saying."

"All you have to do is imprint with her, mate," said Fluke.

Marlin was confused.

"Look her in the eye and say *'Ooo-roo'*, and she'll be in sync with you." Fluke was suddenly very serious. "Now, look her in the eye!"

"Yeah!" added Rudder.

Marlin pulled Nemo aside and the two slinked underwater to speak privately.

"Nemo, I think we should discuss an alternate plan. One that involves staying in the water and with someone sane, because this bird, this bird – this ain't the bird!"

"That's fine, Dad," said Nemo. "And in the meantime, Dory will just forget us. Like you said, it's what she does best."

"Fine," Marlin said with a resigned sigh.

The fish swam to the surface and Marlin cautiously approached Becky. "Look her in the eye," he said to himself. Then he turned towards her. "Which eye?"

"Just pick one, mate," said Fluke.

Marlin tried again. "Becky?"

Becky tilted her head and looked down at him with her crooked eyes. Then she began to coo.

"Roo," said Marlin, trying to speak 'Becky'. *"Ooo-roo."*

Becky squawked. She sidled up next to Marlin and wrapped her wings around him as their lines of vision synced. Nemo laughed while Becky cooed.

"Okay, now, this is all great," said Marlin, spitting out feathers. "But how, exactly, is Becky supposed to carry us?"

"Aw, yeah," said Fluke. "I almost forgot."

Gerald was off in the distance, holding his small bucket in his mouth. Fluke called to him, "Gerald!" With his flipper, he motioned for Gerald to come over.

"Hmmm," Gerald said, looking over at them.

"Yeah! Gerald!" shouted Rudder in a friendly voice.

"Come on, son!" said Fluke. He and Rudder grinned widely.

Gerald hesitated, contemplating.

"Come on, Gerald," said Fluke. "Give us your pail."

Gerald shook his head. "Uhn-uh."

"We'll let you sit on the rock," said Fluke temptingly.

"Yeah, Gerald. We swear it," added Rudder.

Gerald cautiously inched forwards as Fluke and Rudder coaxed him over.

"That's right," said Fluke. "Shimmy on over here."

"C'mon," added Rudder. "You can do it."

"That's right."

"Mind you don't scuff your bum," warned Rudder in a sweet voice.

Gerald giggled happily and put down the bucket as he settled in. He continued to laugh and chuckle as if he were simply too happy to form words.

"Thank you so much, Gerald," said Fluke.

"Welcome to your time on this rock," said Rudder.

"Comfortable, isn't it?" said Fluke.

They sat in silence for a short moment and then Fluke and Rudder lunged at Gerald, yelling in his face. "TIME'S UP! Now get off, Gerald!" shouted Fluke.

"Off! Off! Off! Off!" barked Rudder.

Gerald leaped into the water without his bucket and swam away.

Becky scooped Marlin and Nemo into the bucket with a bit of water.

"This is nuts!" shouted Marlin. "Why do I keep getting talked into insane choices?"

Marlin and Nemo screamed as Becky squawked and flew into the sky, carrying them towards the Institute.

Destiny and Bailey peered across the way, ready and waiting. On the other side of the glass, tourists happily snapped pictures of them. Bailey looked out intensely, waiting for the right moment.

"Okay," he said. "When I tell you you're gonna –"

"Yeah, I got it, okay," said Destiny. "I'm gonna signal with a big splash."

"Not clear yet ..." said Bailey, keeping his eyes focused on the crowd.

Meanwhile, on the other side of the room, Dory and Hank hid in an empty pushchair in the rack.

Dory is excited to be joining Nemo's class on a trip.

Dory wants to be Mr Ray's assistant for the day.

The class is watching the stingray migration.
It's a beautiful sight!

Dory gets knocked out by the stingrays. Mr Ray, Nemo
and the rest of the class peer down at her.

Dory mutters, "Jewel of Morro Bay, California,"
as she wakes up. She remembers something!

With Marlin and Nemo watching, Dory searches
her mind for the hidden memory.

Dory remembers her family! She asks Marlin
and Nemo to go with her to California.

When Dory arrives in Morro Bay, California, she has
some plastic rings caught around her body.

Dory is caught and taken away by some humans in a boat.

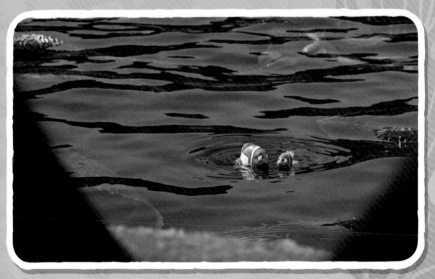

Marlin and Nemo are left in the bay. They must find Dory!

Dory is dropped into a shallow pool
at the Marine Life Institute.

A starfish in the pool yells a warning to Dory.

It's a children's touch pool! A sea creature
gets poked by chubby fingers.

Dory tries to lead Hank the septopus to safety.

Destiny and Bailey talk to Dory, who is lost inside the pipes.

Bailey uses his echolocation to see Dory and
help her find her way to Quarantine.

From inside a toddler's drinking cup on the tray, Dory's eyes darted left and right as she waited for the signal. Hank gobbled up some leftover biscuits in the undercarriage.

"You know something?" he said. "I have no idea why you're even doing this."

"What do you mean?" asked Dory.

"Seems like a lot of trouble just to find some more fish. If I had short-term memory loss, I'd just swim off into the blue and forget everything," Hank admitted.

"But I don't want to do that. I want my family."

"Not me, kid. I don't want anyone to worry about. You're lucky. No memories, no problems."

Bailey watched from the tank as parents parked their pushchairs. "Still not clear ... still not clear."

"You don't have to say when it's not time," said Destiny, irritated.

"Not –" Bailey said again.

"Just tell me when it is time!" said Destiny.

"Okay, here we go ... and ... WAIT!"

"Are you serious!"

"Okay, on the count of three," said Bailey.

"Don't count, just say, 'Go – '"

"GO! NOW! NOW! Do it! Do it!" urged Bailey.

Destiny leaped out of the water, making a giant splash that sent all the gawking tourists scattering and squealing with delight.

"Wow, look at that," said Dory.

"That's the signal!" shouted Hank, reminding her.

"Go, go, go! That's the signal!" repeated Dory.

The pushchair carefully rolled forward and took off, keeping pace among the moving crowd. Hank drove from down below, using his tentacles, while Dory navigated from the toddler's cup.

"Now remember, Destiny said that Deep Sea Drive will take us to Open Ocean," said Hank. "So follow the signs that say Deep Sea Drive."

Dory repeated, "Deep Sea Drive to Open Ocean gets me to my family."

She looked ahead and saw the sign for Deep Sea Drive pointing to the right. Blue tangs were pictured on the banners on the wall. "Go right!"

Hank turned right and kept the pushchair on the side of the pathways, but he couldn't avoid bumping into a couple of people along the way.

"Left!" yelled Dory.

"And steer clear of people, will ya?" Hank called up from the undercarriage. "Especially kids! I don't want to be touched."

"Shhh! Do not mess me up!" said Dory, trying to concentrate. She took her eyes of the road to respond to Hank, but when she looked back, she was heading straight towards a kid holding a bag of popcorn.

"Ahh!" she shouted.

In a last-ditch effort to avoid a crash, Dory and Hank were thrown from the pushchair. Dory, still in her cup, rolled over to some parents. One of the mothers noticed the cup and began walking towards the pushchair. "Oh, poor baby," she said, picking up the cup. "Let me get that for you."

Hank frantically looked around for somewhere to hide. His only choice was to camouflage himself as a human baby before the mother leaned in to return the cup. So he did – and just in time.

"Oh, my," the mother muttered to herself, looking at the strange baby in the pushchair. Hank was a very strange-looking baby indeed. She quickly put the cup in the hands of the 'baby' and turned away. Hank drank from it in an attempt to look more babylike.

"I used to think all babies were cute," the mother said quietly, looking around.

Now that Hank and Dory were reunited, they continued their search.

"Where do we go?" Hank begged.

"Oh. Sorry! Okay, I was looking...." Dory said, panicking.

Up above, Becky flew over the Institute with Marlin and Nemo in the bucket.

"*Roo-roo,* Becky! Drop us anywhere!" said Marlin. "We're okay!"

"Just wait, Dad! I think she's looking for a place to land," said Nemo.

"She's confused, Nemo! She doesn't even know which way to look!"

"*Squawk! Roo-roo?*" said Becky, catching sight of the popcorn spilled and scattered all over the ground.

She suddenly changed course and flew towards a tree. She hung the bucket that contained Nemo and Marlin on a branch, swooped down to the popcorn and began to eat.

Hank and Dory continued in the pushchair, but Dory became confused when they reached a junction. She looked around, puzzled, trying to work out how to make the right choice.

"Which way?" nudged Hank.

Dory's face lit up when her eyes landed on a sign that read THE WORLD'S MOST POWERFUL PAIR OF GLASSES! Next to the sign was an arrow pointing to the left.

"I remember that!" Dory shouted. "We need to go left!"

Unfortunately, she didn't see the sign for Deep Sea Drive, which pointed to the right.

Marlin and Nemo were stranded inside the bucket, hanging from the branch, while Becky fought other birds for kernels of popcorn.

Marlin called to her, but Becky was focused on eating as much popcorn as possible – and she was out of earshot. "We have to get closer to Becky so she can hear us," Marlin said. He nudged the bucket down the branch, in an effort to close the gap between them.

"I don't think we should move the pail," said Nemo.

Marlin continued to nudge. "Nemo, without me, Becky is lost."

"Dad, just trust her."

"Trust her? So she can forget us altogether?"

"I trust Becky," said Nemo.

The bucket moved further down the branch.

"You trust Becky," Marlin said incredulously. "Becky's *eating a cup*!" He gestured in her direction. She had a cup over her head and was turning in circles, looking confused.

"Becky!" Marlin tried calling again. *"Loo-loo!"*

WHIP! Suddenly, the weight of the bucket moving down the branch caused it to fling upwards. It launched Marlin and Nemo out of the bucket and into the sky! Screaming, they landed on an outdoor awning and tumbled into a tank of toy robot fish in the gift shop.

"Well, at least we're not stuck in a bucket anymore," said Marlin.

They watched through the glass of the toy tank as Becky finished eating and flew back to the bucket. She grabbed it and flew to the roof of Quarantine, then peeked into the bucket and squawked, confused.

"Or on top of Quarantine," said Nemo.

Marlin sighed.

12

Dory and Hank pulled up near the sea otter area, where a perky tour guide was talking to a group of excited tourists.

"Looking for the world's most powerful pair of glasses," Dory said as she glanced around. She gasped when she saw the otters swimming in their tank. She couldn't help pausing to watch. They were so cute! The adorable furry otters rolled around in the water happily, clapping their feet and chirping. One otter hugged another and soon they were all hugging and cuddling each other!

"It's a huge cuddle party!" said the guide as the crowd watched adoringly.

"Cuddle party?" Dory gasped. "I'm in!"

From the bottom of the pushchair, Hank looked around, confused. "Wait. Where are we? Are we still on Deep Sea Drive?"

"Uh ... yes, I think – Well, I don't know – but I saw that sign and –" Dory stammered.

"What? What sign?" asked Hank.

"The one about the world's most powerful pair of glasses."

"What are you talking about? Why would we follow that sign?" Hank couldn't believe it!

"Well, um, because I remembered it."

In a panic, Hank emerged from the pushchair slightly. "No, no, no! That wasn't the plan – ow!" Hank screeched as a passing tourist stepped on one of his tentacles.

He dragged the pushchair aside to talk to Dory. "That's it!" he said angrily. "You have wasted my time!"

"Wait, no," said Dory.

"The transport truck leaves at dawn and I'm not missing it! So give me your tag!"

"Wait. Hank, *Hank,* I really think we are on the right path."

"Are you kidding me? You got us completely lost!

The plan was to follow Deep Sea Drive and you couldn't stick to it!"

"Because I saw something – something I remembered – and I was sure that it was –"

"Something you *remembered*?" Hank was furious. "You can't remember anything! It's probably how you lost your family in the first place!"

Dory winced, hurt.

Hank softened, suddenly feeling he had gone too far.

"All right, look. Let's just take it down a notch. Just give me the tag and –"

"You know something? For a guy with three hearts, you're not very nice!"

"Three hearts? What are you talking about? I don't have three hearts."

"Yes, you do," Dory insisted.

"I don't."

"You do!"

"Don't."

"Do."

"Stop saying that!"

Hank noticed the pushchair was starting to roll down a hill. But Dory, busy ranting, did not. "I did not lose my family!" she shouted.

"Whoa, wait!"

"My mum and dad took good care of me and made me feel special," Dory continued. "And I don't know what happened, but I would never lose them. You got that?"

The pushchair rolled into the Kid Zone building and hit the side of a touch-pool display. Hank screamed as they were both launched into the shallow water!

13

"**I** DID NOT LOSE THEM!" Dory shouted. She opened her eyes and saw that she was in a shallow pool. Sand and fake rocks were scattered about and it was eerily quiet. Dory searched for her friend. "Hank?" she called. But there was no answer.

A variety of sea creatures, starfish, anemones and sea cucumbers inched into the shadows. Some closed up tightly, while others tried their best to find somewhere to hide. A frightened sea cucumber burrowing in the sand behind her spoke in a hushed tone. "Hans...."

"No, not Hans, I'm looking for Hank," said Dory.

"HANS," the sea cucumber said a little louder, sinking deeper into the sand.

"Hank with a *K*. HanK. *HanK*," said Dory.

"HANDS!" the sea cucumber said, then it disappeared into the sand.

"Hands? Oh-ho-ho, HANDS!" said Dory.

Suddenly, the deafening sound of excited children echoed from above and tiny hands plunged into the pool. Their little fingers poked and prodded the terrified creatures – it was a nightmare! A chubby little hand grabbed the sea cucumber and yanked it out of its hiding place. While the sea cucumber screamed, the kid shrieked with laughter.

Dory weaved to avoid the hands as she looked for Hank. Creatures everywhere cried out in pain and begged for mercy.

"No! No! Please!" screamed a sea urchin.

"Ow! Aaaah! No! This is not okay! Stop! Please!" screamed a terrified fish.

"My arm!" yelled a starfish.

"Hank, where are you?" Dory dodged more hands, nervously looking everywhere. She spotted a starfish crawling desperately towards a rock cave.

"Can you please help me? I'm looking for –" Dory watched in horror as a hand plunged in and dragged the screaming starfish back into the murk.

"Please help me," Dory said to a sea cucumber who was trying to stay hidden. "I've lost my friend Frank." She paused. "I'm sorry, not Frank."

"You're in my space!" shouted the sea cucumber. Then a hand reached in, grabbed it and pulled it out of the water.

"He's an oc-octopus? No, septopus. That's right, he's a septopus. Septopus, septopus, septopus," she repeated, scrunching up her eyes and patting her fins to her temples in an effort to remember.

Dory suddenly realized – Hank was probably camouflaged! She began to look in a different way and noticed a piece of coral with seven long arms!

"Hank! Come on! Let's get outta here," she said, tugging him to safety.

Hank revealed himself. "Dory, what are you doing?" Terrified, he scrambled under a rock.

Dory raced after him and clung to one of his tentacles. "Hank! What's the plan?"

"The plan is I'm gonna stay here forever!" said Hank, terrified.

"Okay. Good plan," said Dory. She looked out at all the sea creatures, swimming for their lives and screaming in fear.

"I'm sorry, Hank," said Dory genuinely. "I'm sorry I can't remember right."

FLASH! A vivid memory struck Dory again.

She saw her childhood home and her father was calling to her.

"Oh! Watch out, Kelpcake!"

A sunfish passed in front of her as she was pulled back. "Ho, ho!" he said. "Watch where you're going."

Lots of fish traffic passed around the family. She could see the shell path leading all the way from her childhood home into the reef.

"I'm sorry, Daddy," said little Dory. "I'm sorry I can't remember right."

Jenny comforted Dory, speaking softly and gently. "You don't need to be sorry. You know what you need to do? Just ... keep swimming. And I bet you can remember that because we're just ... we're gonna ... um, we're going to sing a song about it." Then her mother began to sing, "Just keep swimming.... Just keep swimming...."

Charlie started to sing along with Jenny and the two went back and forth, singing in silly voices — even operatic! Little Dory giggled and sang along with her parents as they all swam together, singing and having fun.

Just as quickly as it came, the memory vanished and Dory was back in the present moment. "My mum taught me that song! All this time, I thought I'd made it up!" she said, surprised.

"What song?" asked Hank.

"Just keep swimming!" she answered. "Hank, we've just got to keep swimming!"

"What? No way. Listen to me: it's too dangerous to move!"

Dory faced Hank. "No, you listen to me," she said firmly. "This is the only way to survive. I know you're scared, but you can't give up. Follow me!"

Then she pulled him by one of his arms and they creeped out of hiding. It was a total disaster – curious hands seemed to cover every centimetre of the pool!

Finally, a space opened in front of them and Dory raced ahead, singing her song. *"Just keep swimming.... Just keep swimming...."*

Hank screamed as Dory pulled him along. Some sea worms poked their heads through holes in the rocks, giving ominous warnings as the friends passed by.

"Turn back! Turn back! You're heading right for Poker's Cove! Poker's Cove!" they shouted.

Other fish stopped and stared, but it was too late: Dory led them directly into the grubbiest, poking-est place of all.

"Incoming!" yelled a starfish, and all the fish in the touch pool screamed in terror. Dory and Hank panicked as fingers and hands began to poke and grab them!

One excited finger jabbed Hank in his side. Hard. In an instant, Hank inked and the entire touch pool went black!

Disgusted, the children yanked their hands from the pool. "Ew! What is it?" they shouted, running off and crying.

"Sorry," said Hank, embarrassed.

"That's okay, everybody does it. Nothing to be ashamed of," said Dory kindly.

A few seconds passed as Dory anxiously looked around for Hank in the black water. He finally emerged from a far corner of the pool and Dory raced over to him, hugging him tightly. "Hank? Oh, Hank! There you are!"

Hank was stunned. Not only was he not used to being hugged, but he was amazed that they were actually safe. The pool felt a bit eerie now that all the kids had disappeared.

"Wow," he said. "You ... got us out of there."

"I did, didn't I?" Dory couldn't believe it, either. "I got us out of there."

"I mean, technically you also got us in there. But if you hadn't, I'm not sure we would have got – here."

Dory followed Hank's gaze to a display that read ECHOLOCATION ... THE WORLD'S MOST POWERFUL PAIR OF GLASSES!

She gasped. "The world's most powerful pair of glasses. We found it!"

"No, no, no," said Hank, pointing past the display. "You found *THAT*."

The entire wall behind the display opened to reveal the entrance to the Open Ocean exhibit! A massive, cylindrical aquarium filled the entire room. Colourful fish of all different sizes swam around as a crowd of tourists stood stunned, watching the incredible display. Music played and a voice began to speak.

"Hello," said the voice.

It was the voice that Dory had heard before, out in the bay. Dory couldn't believe it.

"Welcome to Open Ocean!"

"Home," Dory whispered.

14

From inside the tank in the gift shop, Marlin called desperately for Becky. *"Loo-loo! Loo-loo!"*

"Dad, stop. She's not coming back," said Nemo.

"She might," said Marlin and he continued to call for her. *"Loo-loo! Loo-loo!"*

"Dad! She's not coming back. Because you made her feel like she couldn't do it," said Nemo. Then he turned away and swam to the bottom of the tank. Marlin swam down to join him.

"You're not talking about Becky, are you?" asked Marlin.

"I miss Dory," said Nemo.

"Me too," said Marlin with a sigh. He came nose to nose with a blue tang robot fish and pushed it away. "Truth is, I'm just so worried about her."

"She's the one who should be worried about us," said Nemo.

"Well, she'd definitely have an idea of what to do if she were here. I don't know how she does that."

"I don't think she knows, Dad. She just ... *does*."

"Well, then, we'll just have to ... think."

They both fell into deep thought for a moment. Then they said simultaneously, "What would Dory do?"

"Yeah, what *would* Dory do?" said Nemo, excited.

"She would assess her situation and then she'd evaluate. Then she would analyse her options –"

Nemo cut him off. "Dad. That's 'What would *Marlin* do?'"

"Right," said Marlin. "That's what I would do. She wouldn't even think twice," Marlin looked around. "She would just look at the first thing she sees and –" He looked out through the glass of the tank and saw a series of fountains outside, across a square. A jet stream of water appeared to jump from one fountain to the next. An idea popped into Marlin's head, but he sighed – could they really do that?

"Dory would do it," said Nemo. He knew what Marlin was thinking.

Marlin took a deep breath and swam to the surface of the water. "Hold on to me!" They leaped out of the tank, bouncing off the top of a nearby pushchair and caught a stream of water as it shot out of the ground.

Like surfers catching wave after wave, the two managed to hop from jet stream to jet stream, making their way across the plaza. It was like flying!

But suddenly, all the jet streams shut off and they plummeted to the ground. They flipped and flopped on the concrete, helplessly gasping for water.

"What ... would Dory ... do," chanted Nemo.

"Just ... keep ... gasping," said Marlin.

Suddenly, a burst of water shot out and carried them high up into the air. All at once, the jet streams had turned on again! Then Marlin and Nemo fell into a shallow outdoor tidal-pool exhibit with a SPLASH!

"Are you okay?" asked Marlin.

"Yeah! What would Dory do now?" asked Nemo.

A voice piped up behind them. "Who's Dory?"

It was a giant clam, attached to the wall of the tank.

"Oh, boy. Are we happy to see you," said Marlin.

"Happy to see me? I'm happy to see you! I haven't had anyone to talk to in years," said the clam.

"Years? Wow. Well, unfortunately, we can't stay long. We have to go because –"

"Now, why would you want to go? You just landed. Stay a while. Tell me all about yourself."

"Well, I would love to, but my son and I have to get to Quarantine, so –"

"Wonderful thing, to have a son," said the clam. He paused for a moment, lost in thought. "Course, I didn't have a family. I dated a nice scallop for a while."

"Well, that's fascinating," Marlin said.

"But scallops have eyes," the clam continued. "And she was looking for something different."

The group shared an awkward silence before the clam continued. "I'm kidding! Well, not about scallops having eyes. They do. And they see into your soul and they break your heart. Oh, Shelley! WHHHHYYYY?" The clam broke down into hysterics, crying and whining, as Marlin and Nemo watched uncomfortably.

Marlin turned to Nemo. "*Now* what would Dory do?"

15

Hank held Dory in a clear plastic cup of water and used a large yellow CAUTION: WET FLOOR sign to hide them as he snuck across the room. The voice continued to speak to the tourists in the Open Ocean exhibit. "Now come with us as we explore the mysterious world of the Open Ocean."

Dory gawked at the exhibit anxiously. "Mum and Dad," she whispered. "They're actually in there."

"Don't celebrate yet," said Hank. "We still have to get you inside that thing."

When it was safe, Hank slithered out of the sign and quickly camouflaged as a continent on a giant globe in the centre of the room. Then he carefully moved closer to the exhibit. As they neared it, Dory started to worry about meeting her parents.

"What do I say to them? I should introduce myself, probably. 'Hi! I'm Dory.'"

Hank jumped up to some banners and swung himself towards a blue whale skeleton. He did a double take when he saw a display that read DID YOU KNOW THE OCTOPUS HAS THREE HEARTS? Hank put it out of his mind and clung to the ribs of the whale skeleton as he swung into the exhibit.

Dory continued to worry. "I mean, we have so much to catch up on. Not that I remember any of it or anything that we did together.... What do you think I should say when I meet them? What if they don't recognize me?" she asked nervously.

Hank grabbed on to a rope that dangled from the ceiling lights, causing a spotlight to swivel over the crowd. One man in the crowd looked up, but Hank flashed the light into his eyes and he quickly covered his face. Hank managed to stay hidden.

"Oh, I should have brought a gift. We just passed a gift shop," Dory said, turning her head towards the store. "Dang it. Why didn't I think of that before?"

Dory continued to ramble as they landed on the Institute's upper scaffolding. Hank ducked out of view to avoid being seen by a passing worker. Once the coast was clear, he peered over the upper platform to the Open Ocean aquarium and lowered himself towards the water.

"Well, looks like this is it, kid. Now I got a truck to catch," said Hank.

"Wait, I had something for you," said Dory.

Hank watched as Dory thought with a blank stare. Hank smiled. "Tag," he said patiently.

"The tag. Right." Dory took it off and handed it to him. Then she looked at him, a little sad. "You know, I think I'm going to remember you," she said sincerely.

"Ah, you'll forget me in a heartbeat, kid," Hank said with a chuckle. "Three heartbeats." He paused for a moment and looked at Dory. "I'll have a hard time forgetting you, though."

Dory looked down at the huge tank of thousands of fish and took a deep breath. She was nervous about trying to find her parents without any help.

"They're actually down there, aren't they?" Dory said. "I hope I can find them."

"Knowing you, I'm liking your chances," said

Hank. "Now go find your family." Then he gently dropped her into the tank.

Dory's heart raced as she looked around the enormous aquarium. Large schools of fish circled, swimming in the same direction. She swam into the rapidly moving crowd and approached some of the passing fish. She asked again and again if they had seen her parents, but none of them were able to offer any clues.

Discouraged, she watched a stream of small fish swirl around her and swim downwards. Her big eyes rested on the Open Ocean floor, where she saw something familiar hidden in the sand: a trail of shells. She gasped and swam down to take a closer look. "Shells ..." she said, remembering.

FLASH! Another memory came to her. But this time it was different. It was as clear as day – she was actually floating *right there*, where the memory had occurred! As it unfolded in her mind, it seemed to happen all around her. It was as if ghosts of her younger self, and Jenny and Charlie, were there with her, playing out the scene. She could see her parents placing shells down in the sand, in a long line right over there. Dory watched, mesmerized. It was like reliving the past.

"Now, if you ever get lost, Dory," Charlie said.

"You just ... follow the shells," said Jenny.

"Hey, look! Shells!" said little Dory, noticing the shells.

Awestruck, Dory swam behind the ghost images as they followed the shells. The trail led through the coral, winding through it until –

Dory spotted a wall of sea grass that she instantly recognized and the ghosts quickly faded into the background. "My home," she said. "THAT'S MY HOME!" She rushed towards it with anticipation. She felt she was just a moment away from finding her parents. "MUM! DAD!" she called. "I'm home!"

As Dory looked at her childhood surroundings, every view triggered another memory. As she came upon the front yard, the ghosts appeared. She watched young Dory and her parents having fun playing hide-and-seek. When Dory looked up at her tube-coral bedroom, she could see little Dory speaking whale through a vent.

But once the memory ghosts faded, Dory looked around, confused and worried, as a terrible thought entered her mind. Where were her parents? She swam through the opening in the grass fence, calling out their names. Then she spotted a purple shell in the sand and another vivid memory overtook her.

Dory watched as the ghosts appeared and played out the scene.

"Mummy look, purple shells!" said young Dory happily.

Jenny and Charlie stopped her just before she reached the shell.

"Sweetie!" said Jenny. "Undertow! Undertow. You have to stay away from the undertow. Right, Charlie?"

Young Dory looked past the shell down a sandy slope, and a strong current rushed past, tugging and bending the sea grass.

"This is very, very important, Dory," said Charlie. "We see the undertow and we say...."

Her parents watched as they waited for a response, but little Dory didn't seem to understand.

As the ghost memory faded, Dory swam towards the purple shell, remembering. "The undertow," she said quietly.

As she swam over to a pipe entrance, another memory was unlocked and the ghosts returned once more.

She saw her younger self singing softly in bed and stopping at the sound of her mother crying.

"Mummy?" little Dory said with concern as she swam over and peeked into her parents' bedroom.

In the bedroom, Jenny was crying and Charlie was

trying to calm her. Even though Dory was perfectly safe, for now, Jenny couldn't shake the feeling that something terrible was about to happen. They had no idea that little Dory was awake and listening in on their conversation. "What's going to happen to her?" Jenny asked through her sobs. "Do you think she can make it on her own, Charlie?"

"Oh, honey. It'll be okay," said Charlie.

Little Dory looked around desperately, searching for a way to make things better. She didn't want her mother to be sad! She spotted a purple shell off in the distance and raced towards it. "Mummy loves purple shells," little Dory whispered.

As she tried to pick up the shell, she heard her parents screaming her name in panicked voices. Little Dory turned to see their fearful faces a moment before the tug of the undertow pulled at her and sucked her into a cave! She screamed for them, but in an instant, the current carried her through the darkness of the cave and out to the other side. Little Dory found herself swimming in the big blue ocean, all alone.

Dory had tears in her eyes when the memory ended and the ghosts faded away for the last time. She couldn't believe it – she had remembered everything. And now she knew how she had got separated from her parents. She looked around, panicked.

"It was my fault," she said, pained. "My parents ... I lost them."

"Where's your tag?" a crab named Carol asked sharply, snapping Dory into the present moment.

"Huh?" Dory asked.

"Your tag? It's missing. That why you're not in Quarantine?" prodded Carol.

Dory looked at her fin, where the tag used to be. "Quarantine?"

"Yeah. That's where they took all the blue tangs. Isn't that right, Bill?" the crab called back to her husband, who was trimming grass with his claws.

"Yep. Being shipped on a truck to Cleveland at the crack o' dawn," said Bill.

"What? No!" said Dory, panicking. "No, my parents are back in Quarantine? They're being shipped to Cleveland? But I just got here!"

"Oh, it's easy to get to Quarantine. You just go through the pipes, honey," said Carol.

Dory turned and looked at the pipe entrance with dread. "Oh, I can't do that."

Carol was confused. "Why not?"

"I'll forget where I'm going and I, and I – can't be someplace where I have nobody to help me."

"Well, then, I guess you're stuck here," said Bill bluntly.

"You're not helping, Bill," Carol said. Then she turned to Dory. "Just go in there if you want to. You'll be fine."

Dory frowned, looking nervously at the pipe. "Could you, uh, could you tell me how to get there? Through the pipes?"

"Sure, honey. It's two lefts and a right. Simple."

As Carol rushed off, Dory patted her fins against her head, trying to plant the directions firmly in her mind. "Okay, two lefts and a right.... I can do this. Two lefts and a right." Floating by the mouth of the first pipe, she closed her eyes tightly as she repeated, "Two lefts and a right" over and over again, trying to find the strength to begin.

Determined, Dory took another deep breath and squeezed through the pipe, chanting to herself. "Two lefts and a right. Two lefts and a right." She continued to repeat those words as she ventured alone into the darkness.

16

"**T**wo lefts and a right," Dory repeated as she turned a corner. "Two lefts and a ... right? Shoot. Left and a right?" It didn't take long for her to get confused and forget her way. "Wait. Did I already take a left?"

Dory began to panic. "Oh, no. It's happening. Okay, hold on, hold on, hold on, hold on." She started swimming again, taking left after left until she found herself in the same spot. "Okay. I'm lost. It's too hard. I can't remember. I'm forgetting everything! I'm gonna be stuck forever in the pipes! The pipes! The pipe pals. Pipe pals? PIPE PALS!"

Destiny and Bailey were chatting through their pool gate as Bailey tried to teach Destiny how to swim.

"And ... swim, swim, swim –" Bailey said in a singsong voice.

Destiny swam by Bailey hesitantly. "Yeah, I don't know about this!" she said.

"Trust me, I won't let you hit anything – wall!" Bailey quickly warned.

Destiny froze in place right before smashing into a wall. "What's the point?" she asked, frustrated. "I'll never learn to get around!"

"Ya better!" coached Bailey. "If you can't do it in here, you'll never do it out in the ocean. Now really focus, okay? Wall!" he warned again.

But it was too late. Destiny's face smashed right into the wall.

Suddenly, a voice echoed through the pipes. "DESTINYYYYY!"

"Dory?" Destiny quickly turned to a nearby pipe. "Hello?"

"I'm lost in the pipes and my parents are in Quarantine!" Dory said in whale.

"Hang on, Dory!" answered Destiny.

Destiny turned to Bailey and tried to convince him to try to his echolocation.

"You know it's broken!" whined Bailey.

"Just stop it and try the '*ooh*' thing Dory talked about, will you?"

"But I don't think I can –"

"Don't bail on me, Bailey!"

Bailey made an O shape with his mouth and gave it a try. "*OooOOOooo-OoooOOOooo-oooOO!*"

But nothing happened, so he stopped trying.

"Come on, Bailey. What did you just tell me, huh? Really focus!" Destiny said encouragingly.

Bailey tried again, but quickly lost steam.

"I feel stupid."

"Bailey," said Destiny sharply.

"Sorry," he said, and he tried again. "*OOOO ooo OOOh* –" Then something clicked. "I'm getting something!" shouted Bailey. It was working! He could see an X-ray-like image of the pipes inside his mind. It was as if he had an internal 3D map that he could control. "*OOOooooo* – here we go! *Oooo* – oh, yes! *OOooo* – this is amazing! *OOooo* – I can see Quarantine! *Ooooo* – I can see everything! And I can see you!"

"He can see you!" Destiny said in whale, through the pipes.

Bailey was overjoyed.

"Bailey!" shouted Destiny, snapping him back to the task.

"Okay! Tell Dory to go left!" he said.

Bailey continued to use his special skill as Destiny guided Dory towards Quarantine. It was working!

Then Bailey sensed something. "*OOoooo* – I'm light-headed! *Ooooo* – wait! *Oooo OOOoo* –"

"What?" asked Destiny, concerned.

Bailey gasped. "Holy Neptune! She's not alone!" He didn't know what it was, but he could see something moving towards Dory!

"Swim! Swim the other way!" Destiny shouted.

In a panic, they tried to get Dory to swim away from the moving figure, but she kept heading straight for it!

"No! Dory! Turn around!" shouted Destiny.

Bailey covered his eyes. "Oh, I can't look!"

"Aaahh!" Dory screamed.

"Aaahh!" Destiny and Bailey screamed.

Then, in the pipes, Dory heard something entirely unexpected. "Dory?" shouted a pair of voices.

It was Marlin and Nemo!

As the two clown fish wrapped her in a giant hug, Bailey started to cry. *"Ooo* it's consuming her! It's eating her alive!" To him, it looked as though the 'creature' was chomping down on Dory!

In the pipes, Nemo was so happy to see his friend. "You're okay!" he said.

"You found me! How did you find me?" asked Dory.

"There was a crazy clam. He wouldn't stop talking –" Marlin began.

"And we just slowly backed away from him and into these pipes. And then we started looking."

Destiny's whale voice echoed through the pipes. "Dory! I'm sorry!" she half shouted, half cried.

Marlin gasped. "Okay, what was that?"

"Hang on, I gotta take this," Dory said. Then she called in whale, "It's okay! Sorry for what?"

Hearing Dory's voice, Destiny and Bailey celebrated. She was alive!

"I found Marlin and Nemo!" Dory said in whale.

"Dad! Did you hear that? Dory really does speak whale!" Nemo shouted.

"I heard it. And it's bringing back some very bad memories, so let's get outta here," said Marlin, looking around for a way out. "I say we ... we should go this way. Follow me. It's time to head home!"

Marlin started off and Dory followed, but then stopped short. "Wait ... um ... um ... my parents are here," said Dory. Marlin and Nemo couldn't believe she had found them!

"Well, not *here* exactly," Dory explained. "I mean, but, um, I know where they are and I don't know exactly how to get there, but I know what – well, I'm getting help –"

Destiny called through the pipes. "Down to Quarantine."

"Quarantine. That's it!" said Dory.

Dory led the way as Marlin and Nemo followed. They swam along and Dory thought about all the memories that had been coming back to her.

"Do you think my parents will want to see me?" she asked.

"What? Why wouldn't they want to see you?" asked Nemo.

"Because ... I lost them," Dory admitted.

"Dory, your parents are going to be overjoyed to see you. They miss ... everything about you," said Marlin.

"Really?"

"Dory, do you know how we found you?" Marlin asked.

"Something about a clam? Or –"

"No," said Marlin.

"No, an oyster," said Dory.

"No.

"Something?"

"No clam," said Marlin, reaching a fin out to her. "We were having a very hard time until Nemo thought, 'What would Dory do?'"

"Why would you say that?" asked Dory.

"Because ever since I met you, you've shown me how to do stuff I've never dreamed of doing. Crazy things! Outsmarting sharks and jumping jellyfish ... and finding my son. You made all that happen."

"Really? I didn't know you thought that ... unless I forgot."

Marlin sighed. "No, you didn't forget. I never told you. And I'm sorry about that. But Dory, because of who you are, you are about to find your parents. And when you do that ... you'll ... you'll be home," said Marlin, fighting back tears.

Dory and Marlin smiled at each other as they continued to swim along the pipes.

"Dad," Nemo said, quietly pulling Marlin aside. "Does this mean we have to say goodbye to Dory?"

"Yes, Nemo. We do."

At the loading dock inside Quarantine, workers lined up tanks of fish, preparing to load them onto the transport truck.

Dory and Nemo swam out of the pipes and into one of the tanks. They helped pull Marlin through the vent and immediately surveyed their surroundings. They could see everything in the room through the tank's glass.

Dory gasped when she saw a tank of blue tangs at the opposite end of the room, lined up and ready to be loaded onto the moving truck!

"MY FAMILY! C'mon, let's go!" shouted Dory. She leaped from tank to tank, forcing Marlin and Nemo to follow her. "I'm coming, Mummy.... I'm coming, Daddy!"

But just as they were about to dive into the tank of blue tangs, the workers lifted it away! The friends hit the glass and fell into a mop bucket on the floor.

Before they could think of what to do next, three octopus arms reached into the bucket and lifted them out. They screamed in terror and then gasped for breath.

Thankfully, the octopus arms belonged to Hank! He quickly put the friends in a coffeepot full of water.

Dory quickly introduced Hank to Marlin and Nemo, then rushed into the task at hand. "Hank, we need to get in that tank," said Dory. "That rhymed."

"Why?" asked Hank.

"Her parents are there!" said Nemo.

Hank sighed and carried them towards the tank of blue tangs. He was worried they wouldn't make it in time.

"Look, you've got three minutes to get everyone in here with you. Got it?" asked Hank.

"Got it," said Dory.

Hank dumped Dory, Nemo and Marlin in with

the rest of the fish. Twenty blue tangs – all wearing tags – turned and looked at them, surprised.

"Oh, boy," said Dory, taking a deep breath. "Mum? Dad? Oh, boy. Hey, everyone. It's me, Dory!"

The blue tangs murmured with surprise. "Dory? Is it really her? You mean the little forgetful fish?"

"Mum? Dad?" Dory said, looking around, swimming and searching each face. "Where are my parents?" she asked.

The blue tangs lowered their eyes and looked at one another awkwardly. Finally, one of them broke the uncomfortable silence. "Dory? Are you really Jenny and Charlie's girl?"

"Yes, I am! Where are they?"

"Well, right after you disappeared, they thought you must have ended up in Quarantine."

Outside the tank, workers started loading tanks onto the truck. Hank was getting antsy. "C'mon, c'mon, c'mon," he said to himself.

"And so they came here to look for you and –"

"They're here? Where are they?" she shouted, looking around wildly.

"Dory, that was years ago," the fish explained.

"Years ago?" asked Dory.

Marlin looked down. "Oh, no," he said quietly.

"You see, Dory ... when fish don't come back from Quarantine, it means ... they're not ..."

The blue tang tried to work out a kind way to say it. He had hoped that Dory would understand, but she didn't seem to be getting it.

"Dory," Marlin said softly. "They're gone."

Dory's vision became blurry and a lump formed in her throat.

"They're ... dead?" she asked in disbelief.

"They wanted to find you –" said another blue tang.

"Are you sure they're gone?" asked Nemo.

"Dory, listen, it's going to be okay," offered Marlin.

"They loved you so much," said another blue tang.

Hank knocked on the glass and leaned over the top of the tank. He pointed at the workers loading the tanks onto the truck. "Anyone not looking to go to Cleveland, final warning!"

Nemo and Marlin tried to comfort Dory, but she wasn't very receptive.

"I was too late," said Dory sadly.

"Dory, no.... Now listen," started Marlin.

"I don't have a family," she said, on the verge of tears.

"No, that's not true," said Nemo.

"Time to go!" Hank shouted as he watched the forklift slip beneath the blue tang tank.

Dory slowly backed into the coffeepot. "I'm … I'm all alone," she said.

One second before the tank was lifted, Hank yanked up the coffeepot. "Where is everybody else?" he asked. Behind him, the tank was lowered onto the truck. "Your orange friends are on their way to Cleveland!" said Hank.

Suddenly, a giant hand grabbed Hank and he dropped the coffeepot. "Aha! I found the octopus!" said a female worker.

Hank slapped at her with one of his tentacles until she released him into a nearby tank. He instantly camouflaged himself. "Ugh. Where did he go?" she said, annoyed.

From the tank, Hank watched in horror as Dory spilled out onto the floor and down a drain marked TO OCEAN.

18

Dory zipped through the pipes until she finally shot out into the dark, empty ocean. Panting, she helplessly called for her parents. "Mummy! Daddy!"

Searching for help, she raced up to a nearby fish. "Can you help me? I've lost them."

"Lost who?" asked the fish.

"Um ... I ... I," said Dory.

"Sorry, honey. I can't help you if you don't remember," said the fish, swimming off.

Dory looked around desperately and swam up to every fish she saw, asking for help, but she couldn't remember enough for anyone to offer any assistance.

With each fish who turned her down, she became more and more frantic. Finally, feeling like there was nothing more she could do, she began to cry.

"I've lost ... everyone," Dory said to herself. She headed out towards the open water, feeling hopeless and blaming herself for everything that had gone wrong. Her face crinkled as she thought about how she was always so forgetful and how that seemed to cause all her trouble. And even in that moment, the memories she so wanted to hold on to seemed to be slipping away. "I just forget. I forget ... and I forget," she muttered, scolding herself. "I've lost ... something. Something important. What do I do? What do I do? What do I do?"

Suddenly, Dory stopped. "What would Dory do?" The sound of that phrase made her pause. She took a few deep breaths to calm down. "I would ... look around," she said nervously, glancing up and down at her surroundings. "And ... um ... there's just water over there. And a lot of kelp over here. Kelp is better.... Okay." She swam towards the kelp forest. "Okay ... now what? Lots of kelp.... It looks the same. It all looks the same, except there's a rock ... over there. And ... and some sand this way. I like sand. Sand is squishy."

Something caught her eye. It was a shell. She swam towards it and noticed more shells. They were all lined up in the sand, forming a path.

She curiously followed the shells until they led her to a little home made out of an old tyre. Paths of shells led out from the house in every direction. "Wow!" Dory said, looking at all the neatly lined paths stretching out, far and wide. She swam into the tyre, looking for its owners. "Hello?" she called. She swam around and continued to explore. Then she saw two fish off in the distance. She swam towards them, calling out, "Hello. I'm –" When she got close enough to see their faces, she was speechless. It was her mum and dad!

"Dory!" they shouted and rushed to her, smothering her with kisses and hugs.

"You're here.... You're really here.... You found us.... My missing girl.... You're here," said Jenny.

"Dory! Oh, my baby! Let me look at you. I'm never letting you go again!" shouted Charlie.

"It's you," Dory finally said. "It's really you." She couldn't believe it!

The family hugged each other tightly and Dory burst into tears. Then she began apologizing. "I know I've got a problem," she said through tears. "I know and I'm so sorry. And all this time I've wanted to fix it and I can't." Her parents watched with sympathy and understanding as she struggled to find the right words. "And I try – I try. But my thoughts – they leave my head and ideas change. And I forgot you ... and I'm so sorry."

"Dory, Dory, Dory," said Jenny. "Don't you dare be sorry! Look ... look what you did!"

"What?" asked Dory, trying to stop her tears.

"You found us!" exclaimed Charlie, overjoyed.

"That's right! You found us!" said Jenny.

"I did?"

"Oh, honey, you found us. And you know why you found us? Because you remembered. You remembered in your own amazing Dory way."

"Why do you think we never gave up after all these years? And started making paths for you to find? Because we believed one day you'd find us again," said Charlie.

"Exactly!" said Jenny.

"But ... I thought you were gone," said Dory. "How did you –"

Jenny and Charlie explained what had happened all those years before, after Dory disappeared. They went to Quarantine to look for her and when she wasn't there, they figured she must have gone through the pipes. So they left the Institute and had been waiting for her to find them ever since.

"We thought you might come back. And every day, we lay out –"

"Shells," said Dory, touched.

Jenny held Dory's face lovingly in her fins. "And you found us."

"I did," said Dory. "All by myself."

"Oh, honey. Really?" said Charlie. "Have you been by yourself all these years?"

"My poor little girl," said Jenny.

"Oh, I haven't been all by myself," Dory shouted. "Marlin and Nemo!"

19

Marlin and Nemo swam frantically inside their tank on the truck, feeling helpless and worried. Then Nemo thought he spotted Dory floating inside the last tank being carried onto the truck!

Marlin and Nemo were thrilled until Hank uncamouflaged, revealing that it was just one of his tentacles that he'd masked to look like Dory. Marlin was confused. "Hey, where's Dory? Is she with you?"

Hank could barely look at them. "I'm sorry. I tried to hold on, but I couldn't. I lost her," he said.

"All right, let's get going," said one of the workers. "We're going to be late." Nemo and Marlin's faces fell as the back door of the truck slammed shut.

Meanwhile, Dory was racing through the water, talking a mile a minute, trying to fill her parents in on everything that had happened over the years. Dory paused, trying to remember which way to go.

Then she heard a familiar voice over a loudspeaker saying, "Hello."

"There!" shouted Dory, swimming up to the surface. "That's the Marine Life Institute!"

"Oh, you were born there," said Jenny nostalgically.

"Dory, is that where your friends are?" asked Charlie.

"Yes! They were stuck in something ... that was going somewhere ..." said Dory, trying to remember.

Then they heard the roar of a truck starting up in the parking lot above them.

"A TRUCK!" gasped Dory. "They're in the truck!"

Dory immediately began to pace, trying to come up with an idea. Her parents watched, concerned, as she swam around in circles, muttering to herself.

They knew it was nearly impossible for a few fish to stop a moving truck. But Dory continued to rack her brain, searching for a solution. "This has been brought to you by ... echolocation ... echolocation! The world's most powerful ... ocean friends ... friends. Friends ... friend! Destiny. Destiny? Destiny!"

Inside Destiny's pool, a new worker dumped in a bucket of feed and sang, "Time for breakfast, girl!"

Destiny awoke with a snort and swam around the pool, bumping into walls along the way. As she rubbed the sleep from her eyes, she heard a faint, familiar voice cry, *"DESTINYYYYY!"* She quickly swam over to the pipe vent.

"Dooooorrryy?" Destiny answered.

Bailey swam over to the gate, newly awake. "Morning, Destiny," he said with a yawn.

Destiny shushed him. "It's Dory! Something's wrong!"

Bailey and Destiny rose to the surface of their pools. Bailey tapped into his echolocation and began to look for Dory. *"Ooooooo.... I got her! She's right outside the Institute!"*

Bailey told Destiny they had to jump over the wall so they could go into the ocean and help Dory.

"No time to argue!" he said firmly. But Destiny was afraid because of her blurry vision. She didn't think she would survive in the ocean.

"I will be your eyes," Bailey said wisely.

Destiny wasn't so sure.

"But the walls!" she exclaimed.

"There are no walls in the ocean!" Bailey said. Then he leaned in close and whispered in her ear, "It's your destiny, Destiny."

"Well, why didn't you say so?" Destiny dived under the water and raced towards the edge of the pool.

"What? No! Destiny, wait!" yelled Bailey. "No! THAT'S A WALL!"

Destiny shrieked and leaped over the wall just before she crashed! Bailey followed her, jumping out of his own tank with a splash. She and Bailey both landed on the other side. They were now in the ocean – and right next to Dory and her parents.

20

Everybody quickly introduced themselves, but Dory wanted to stay on-task. "We gotta go," she said. "We have to stop that truck!"

When everyone floated up to the surface, they saw that the truck was gone!

Dory gasped. "Bailey! Status report!" she shouted.

"Oh, yes – my beautiful gift!" Bailey snapped into action with his echolocation. "*Ooooo....* I've got it!" he said. He could see the truck!

"Let's go!" said Dory, grabbing Destiny's fin. "We're stopping that truck!" The group took off together and swam past Fluke and Rudder, who were lounging on their rock.

"This I've got to see," said Fluke. Rudder agreed and the two curious sea lions jumped into the water to follow. They didn't get very far before they sensed someone behind them. When they turned around, they saw Gerald – perched on top of their rock and grinning from ear to ear! Fluke and Rudder paused as they considered turning back to scare him off, but they didn't want to miss seeing what was going to happen with Dory and the truck.

"Don't get used to it, Gerald!" shouted Rudder as the two continued on. Gerald laughed wildly and settled onto the beautiful, warm rock.

As the group raced along the coastline, Dory asked Bailey to give her an update. She had already forgotten everything!

Bailey caught her up and then announced that he could see Marlin and Nemo inside the truck ... and it was heading towards the bridge. But he was quickly distracted. "Oh, look! There's a bunch of cute otters over there. I want one!" he added, gazing at the adorable sight. The distraction caused Bailey to slam into the side of the bridge, with Destiny crashing right behind him!

Everyone rose to the surface to have a look around.

"I see the truck!" shouted Charlie. "It's over there!"

The truck was quickly making its way towards the bridge. Dory thought about what to do next. She patted her fins against her head as she chanted, "What would Dory do?" over and over.

"If only there was a way to stop traffic!" said Bailey with a sigh.

"Stop traffic?" repeated Dory. That sparked something in her mind and she chattered as an idea began to form. "Everyone needs to stop ... people stop to look at things ... things they like ... things that are cute ... things that are *cute*!"

Dory turned to the group of sea otters and darted towards them. She told Destiny her plan. "When the truck reaches the bridge, you flip me up there."

"Got it!" said Destiny.

"You guys follow me," Dory said to the otters. They chirped in agreement. "Everyone else, stay here."

"Whoa," said Jenny, stopping Dory. She and Charlie didn't like the idea at all. They didn't want to let Dory out of their sight. "Dory, sweetie, what happens if ... I mean, what could happen if ..." Jenny's voice trembled with worry.

"I lose you again?" asked Dory.

Jenny was ashamed to admit it, but that was her fear.

"Mum, Dad," said Dory, facing them with confidence. "It's gonna be okay. Because I know that even if I forget ... I can find you again."

Jenny and Charlie smiled. They were so proud of their daughter. They knew Dory was right and they would always stand behind her, no matter what.

With no time to waste, Destiny hoisted Dory up onto her tail while Bailey told Destiny which way to aim. "*Ooooo* – Okay, a little left.... *OOoooo* – Okay, that's it.... Go! *Don't* do it!"

"Bailey!" said Destiny, anxiously.

"Okay, NOW! NOW! DO IT! DO IT!"

Destiny swam over to Dory. "Time for your idea," she said.

"Okay, what idea?" asked Dory. Instantly, Destiny flipped Dory high into the air and flung her across the ocean. With Dory soaring above, the otters followed in the water below. They scrambled up onto the bridge and when Dory finally landed, one of them caught her in its paws! They were now lined up across the highway.

Dory looked at all the cars on the bridge and her mind raced. "Cars, cars, cars. I see cars. Otters in front of the cars ... cars have to stop –" Then she remembered her plan. "STOP TRAFFIC! CUDDLE PARTY!"

Dory hugged the otter that was holding her and with that, all the otters began to hug each other. The extreme cuteness caused every single car to stop! All the drivers and passengers stared and snapped photos as the otters had an absolutely adorable cuddle party!

SCREEEECH! The truck lurched to a halt as it approached the traffic jam. Inside the truck, Nemo asked Marlin what was going on and Marlin drew in a deep breath. "I don't know how, I don't know in what way – but I think this has something to do with –"

The truck's back door burst open and an otter scurried in, carrying Dory.

"DORY!" said Nemo.

"Water ... water ..." gasped Dory, straining to catch her breath.

Hank reached down, grabbed Dory and plunged her into the tank with Marlin and Nemo.

"You came back!" Nemo continued.

"Of course," said Dory. "I couldn't leave my family."

Overjoyed, Nemo hugged Dory with all his might. Suddenly, the driver appeared at the open door, shooing the otters out of the truck and off the bridge. "Oh, no," Dory said ominously as she watched the otters return to the ocean. "There goes our ride."

From below, Destiny called to Dory in whale. "The traffic is starting to *mooOOoove*!"

"Leave it to me," said Marlin. "I got this!" He cleared his throat and began to call to Becky. *"Loo-loo! Loo-loo! Ooo-roo!"*

Becky squawked and appeared, holding the bucket in her beak.

"Dory, follow me!" said Marlin. He and Nemo hopped into the bucket, but Becky took off before Dory was able to get in! Marlin tried to get Becky to turn around, but she continued on her mission. She dropped them into the ocean and flew off, joining her flock.

When Marlin and Nemo splashed into the water, they found themselves face to face with Destiny. "AHHH! PLEASE DON'T EAT US!" begged Marlin.

"Where's Dory?" asked Destiny.

Then everyone realized ... "You're her family," they said in unison.

"She's still in the truck!" Marlin announced.

With no time to waste, Marlin managed to get

Becky's attention and told her to go back for Dory. When she arrived at the truck, Hank and Dory were talking.

"Okay, kid," said Hank. "I guess this is goodbye." He reached one of tentacles into her tank, in an effort to put her into Becky's bucket.

"No!" she shouted, slapping his arm.

"What do you mean, no?"

"I mean, you're not going to the Cleveland. You're coming to the ocean with me," Dory insisted.

"What is it with you and ruining my plans?" said Hank. "Listen to me, I have one goal in life, one! And it is to –"

"No, you listen to me!" Dory said firmly. Hank looked at her, stunned by her confidence. "What is so great about plans? I've never had a plan. Did I plan to lose my parents? No. Did I plan to find Marlin? No. Did you and I plan to meet? Wait – did we?"

"Are you almost done?" asked Hank.

"Well, I don't think we did and that's because the best things happen by chance, because that's life. And that's you being with me – out in the ocean, not safe in some stupid glass box."

"Can I say something?" asked Hank.

"I'm not done! A friend of mine once told me

that all it takes is three simple steps – rescue, rehabilitation and, um, one other thing that...."

All the fish in the truck chanted, "RELEASE! RELEASE! RELEASE!"

"That's right! So what do you say?"

Even Becky joined in the chant, squawking along with everyone!

"I was going to say okay," said Hank.

But suddenly the worker appeared and slammed the door shut, leaving them trapped inside the truck.

"Not good," said Dory.

21

In the ocean, everyone panicked when they saw the truck drive over the bridge and away from the water!

"Quick! Guys, grab my fin!" Destiny urged.

Jenny, Charlie, Marlin and Nemo grabbed hold of Destiny as she took off, swimming at full speed along the coastline with Bailey by her side.

Using his echolocation, Bailey could see Hank struggling with the back door of the truck. "He's trying to get the door open! *OoooOooOo* – It's locked from the outside!"

With Bailey focused on Hank, nobody realized that Destiny was about to swim into a bank of land!

All of a sudden, Bailey caught a glimpse of their surroundings and warned Destiny just in time.

"Wall! Wall! Wall!" he shouted.

Destiny screamed but managed to avoid a collision. The group watched sadly as the truck drove out of sight.

"Oh, no-no-no!" Jenny cried.

Destiny asked Bailey where they were headed. "*Oooooo* – I'm losing 'em!" he said.

Inside the truck, Hank had finally given up on the door. He climbed into the tank with Dory. "It's over," he said.

"No," said Dory. "There's got to be a way." She looked around, frantically searching for an idea. Even though Hank doubted her, Dory continued to think.

"There's ALWAYS a way!" she said, getting in Hank's face.

"There isn't, Dory, I'm telling you. This time there is no other way!"

"Hmm, what about that?" said Dory, pointing up to a vent in the roof of the truck.

"Holy carp," said Hank. "There is another way."

Dory was ecstatic! The fish in the truck chanted and cheered as Hank climbed over the tanks, holding Dory, making his way towards the vent.

"RELEASE! RELEASE! RELEASE!" they sang.

Somehow, some way, Hank and Dory squeezed through the vent!

A moment later, the driver and worker screamed when Hank stretched and plastered himself across the windshield! "Get it off! What is it? Get rid of it!" they screamed.

The driver slammed on the brakes and pulled over. The two jumped out and checked the windshield – but Hank was gone!

"What the – ?" said the driver, confused.

SLAM! The truck doors shut and a tentacle reached up, pushing down the locks. The humans were now locked out. Hank was in the driver's seat and Dory swam happily in a Big Gulp cup nearby.

"Suck it, bipeds," said Hank with a chuckle.

"All right, Hank! You've got seven arms. Just – I dunno. Try something!" said Dory, curiously eyeing all the various truck parts.

Hank chuckled nervously as he began to push buttons and pull levers. The horn honked loudly, making the driver and worker jump. One of the levers caused the gas tank door to pop open and another made the lights flash. The two humans stood there watching, dumbfounded. Finally, Hank managed to put the truck into gear – and it started to roll forward.

"Good job, Hank!" cheered Dory.

The driver and worker stayed close, trying to keep up on foot. But when the truck swerved, they had to jump out of the way.

"Can't this thing go any faster?" asked Dory.

Hank tried one of the pedals on the floor and the truck came to an abrupt stop. When he tried another, the engine revved and the truck surged forward. The worker and driver stood in shock, watching the truck speed away!

Dory shouted out directions as Hank steered. But when they passed the two humans again, they knew they had driven in a circle!

"Turn right!" shouted Dory. "Back to the ocean!"

SCREECH! The truck made a U-turn and was heading straight for the humans! The two leaped out of the way to avoid being hit. Once again, the truck raced off, leaving the stunned driver and worker in the dust!

"We are so fired," muttered the driver, catching her breath.

As Dory continued to navigate, the truck weaved in and out of traffic, causing other cars to swerve.

Dory smiled at Hank as he turned the wheel this way and that. "Good driving, Hank!"

"Pay attention to the road!" Hank said.

"Oh, I'm sorry," said Dory. Up ahead she could see that the road split off in different directions. Her eyes darted around as she tried to work out which way to go. Finally, she spotted a car pulling a boat.

"Right! Boats go to the ocean!" Dory exclaimed.

The fish in the back of the truck were jostled around as Hank made a sharp right turn. Then Dory got a closer look at the driver of the car pulling the boat. He was sunburned and had sand all over his feet. Her mouth dropped open. "He's already been to the ocean! Turn around!" she urged.

In the ocean, Marlin and the crew were losing hope. "My sweet little Kelpcake!" said Charlie though tears.

"Where is she?" said Jenny as she wept.

Bailey was trying to locate Dory. "*OoOOOOoo* – Oh wait! *Oooo* – Hold on. *OoooOOo* – I'm getting something!" he said excitedly.

"Is it them? Is everything perfect?" asked Destiny.

22

"Just perfect," said Hank sarcastically as he eyed the gas tank. It was almost empty. "We're nearly out of time, kid. Where do we go now?"

"Uh ... I don't see anything," said Dory, trying to work out how to find the ocean.

SPLAT! Dory gasped as a white liquid splattered on the windshield. A flock of seagulls flew overhead! They continued along, flying across the horizon to the left, screeching, "Mine! Mine! Mine!"

Dory gasped. "Seagulls.... The ocean's left, Hank!"

Hank pulled left and they drove up a steep hill. When they got to the top, they could see it! "The ocean!" shouted Dory. "It's straight ahead. Floor it!"

Then Dory noticed police cars blocking their way. "Uh-oh."

"What do you mean, uh-oh?" asked Hank.

Dory looked around, figuring out their next move. Then she gasped. "Hank! I'm going to ask you to do something crazy."

Hank smiled. "I'm okay with crazy."

Bailey gave everyone the news. "*Ooo Ooooo* – there's no way out! It's over! They're going to fish jail!" Then his expression changed. "*Oooo* – wait.... *OOoo OO* – oh, no ... *ooo*, GET BACK!" He screamed and pushed everyone out of the way. "INCOMING!"

They heard the deep sound of a blaring horn from above and looked up to see the truck hanging off the side of a rocky cliff. Then it dived off and fell straight towards the ocean!

As the truck tumbled through the air, the fish inside screamed, cheered and laughed as their tanks slid out of the open back door. Becky fell out and happily squawked as she sailed through the air inside the green bucket.

From their rock, Fluke and Rudder looked up, amazed, as the fish rained down. They opened their mouths wide, waiting for something tasty to fall in. While they were distracted, Gerald creeped up between them and shoved them off the rock. He sat triumphantly and caught the bucket holding Becky with his mouth.

When Dory and Hank finally fell out of the truck, they could hear the voice over the loudspeaker: "What lies before you represents the third and final part of the Marine Life Mission: rescue, rehabilitation and release."

They shared a smile as they continued to descend towards Dory's families waiting below.

"Come to Papa!" shouted Charlie.

They finally plunged into the ocean water as a victorious explosion of bubbles rose up around them.

23

Back home on the Great Barrier Reef, Dory was counting. "One, two, three ... four ... um? Wait a minute. Why am I counting?" Dory removed her fins from her eyes and looked around. "Where is everyone? Uh-oh. Did they leave me? No, most likely not. Come on." She started to swim around the reef.

"Okay, well, it's okay. I can figure this out," she said confidently. "What was I doing just now? Um ... I was – Okay, why was I covering my face? Why was I trying to hide? Hide. Hide! Wait, I know!" She continued to count. "Five, six, seven, eight, nine, ten! Ready or not, here I come!"

Dory searched around the reef and found all her hiding family members and friends. The fish from Nemo's class laughed as she found each one. "All right, you little shrimps, recess is over," said Hank. The kids were disappointed, but gathered in front of Hank. "Bring it in. Time for another lesson."

"When is Mr Ray coming back from his migration?" asked Chickenfish.

"If he's smart, he'll stay away from here as long as he can. But until he does, I'm your substitute teacher," said Hank. "All right, give your full attention to Mr Bailey here."

Hank gestured to Bailey, who was beaming with pride.

"Thank you so much, Mr Hank. Okay, kids, who wants to learn about echolocation?"

The kids booed and Bailey's smile fell.

"Hey, c'mon, guys," said Destiny. "It's actually really cool."

"What are you supposed to be?" asked Chickenfish.

"I'm glad you asked," said Destiny. "I'm a whale shark. And if I could see you, I'd eat you all in one bite!"

"Cool!" cheered the class. Then they chanted, "Do it! Do it! Do it!"

Outside the classroom, Dory faced Marlin, Jenny and Charlie. "I'll see you in a little while, guys. I've got something I want to do," she said.

"Okay, Kelpcake," said Charlie. "Have fun!"

"Family swim when you get back!" said Jenny.

Marlin watched Dory as she swam away. "It's so nice that Dory can go off by herself. She'll always know how to find her way home. Never have to worry again," he said.

Dory swam along, happily humming, "Just keep swimming...."

But after keeping such a close eye on her for so long, Marlin couldn't let Dory be alone. He peered out from behind some coral, secretly trailing behind her. He watched as she changed direction and followed closely, trying to stay out of view. He saw Dory head towards the edge of the reef and it didn't take long before he started to panic.

"Dory, no," Marlin whispered.

Then she settled at the very edge of the drop-off. Dory just floated, staring out at the vast blue ocean beyond the reef. "Hey, Marlin," she said, without turning around.

Marlin swam over and joined her. "Oh, hey. Hello, Dory," he said, trying to sound normal.

"You all right? You look worried," said Dory.

"Oh, I'm fine. It's – how I always look."

"I was just enjoying the view," said Dory, smiling.

They both stared out into the peaceful open water, happy to be together.

"Wow," said Marlin. "It really is quite a view."

"Yup."

Marlin looked back in the opposite direction, towards the reef and smiled. "So is this one."

Dory turned to see what he was looking at. Her big eyes lit up and her smile widened. She saw her new, combined family floating together at the edge of the reef. Her parents were there – along with Nemo, Hank, Destiny and Bailey. It's true, they were all different kinds of sea creature. But now, because of Dory, they were important parts of one incredible family.

"Unforgettable," she said.